Creatures

Once I Caught a Fish Alive

"It *is* bigger," Gemma said uneasily. "In fact, I'd say it's grown about three centimetres since yesterday."

Paul didn't answer. He dared not, because he agreed with her and didn't want to acknowledge it. The fish gazed back through the glass and fanned its tail and fins lazily. They had both been trying to outstare it, but had found they couldn't; the fish had a patience and determination that was unnerving, and it simply wouldn't look away. Paul thought: *It's challenging us. It knows we're getting the wind up, and it's enjoying every moment. What sort of creature have I landed myself with?*

**Look for other Creatures titles
by Louise Cooper:**

Creatures

Once I Caught a Fish Alive

Louise Cooper

Hippo

Scholastic Children's Books
Commonwealth House, 1–19 New Oxford Street,
London WC1A 1NU, UK
London ~ New York ~ Toronto ~ Sydney ~ Auckland
Mexico City ~ New Delhi ~ Hong Kong
First published by Scholastic Ltd, 1998

ISBN 0 590 11162 0

Typeset by Falcon Oast Graphic Art
Printed by Cox & Wyman Ltd, Reading, Berks

10 9 8 7 6 5 4 3 2 1

For James
Who said "spooks" and "animals" in
the same breath, and so opened the
door of the cage!

1

"Win a fish! Win a luvly, lively little fish!"

You could hear the bawling voice halfway across the field, above all the shrieking and clanging and banging and blaring music of the fair. Gemma's heart sank. The moment Paul, her brother, heard the word "fish", he'd be hooked. In fact, when she looked at him she saw that she was already too late. Paul *had* heard, and his ears – Gemma would have sworn it, she really would – pricked up.

"Come on, Gem! I'm going to see if I can win one!"

"It's only a hoop-la stall," Gemma protested. "Really *boring*. Why don't we go on the dodgems again, or——"

But Paul was already heading towards the booth. Reluctantly Gemma followed, grumbling: "OK, OK; go and win a fish, and then maybe we can have some fun. *If* there's any fun to be had," she added grouchily.

If Paul wanted her opinion, this May Bank Holiday fair was a complete let-down. It was too small, too old-fashioned, there weren't any half-way decent rides, and the prizes at the stalls were trashy. Who wanted a chipped plaster puppy, or a bottle of bath stuff that smelled worse than Mum's air-freshener? She had only come at all because it was too cold to go to the beach, and now she wished she hadn't bothered.

Paul ignored her. The hoop-la stall was in sight now and he stopped and stared in astonishment. The owner was a squat, dumpy little man, like a barrel on two incredibly bandy legs, and with a very long nose down which his pale-blue eyes squinted. As for his clothes. . . His jacket was even louder than his voice, patterned with multicoloured fish. It clashed horribly with his check trousers, and they in turn clashed horribly with his headgear – a tweed fisherman's hat, decorated all over with fake flies.

As Paul stared, the stallholder saw him and grinned. The grin was hideous, for he had huge teeth that looked as if they had been filed down to points. In fact, Paul thought, what with the teeth and the nose and the eyes, he looked exactly like a shark.

But there was nothing sharklike about his greeting.

"Hello, son!" he bawled with gusty cheerfulness. "Going to try your luck at winning a fish, then?"

He held up a polythene bag full of water. A fish was swimming around in it, and Paul's eyes lit up. He had expected an ordinary goldfish, like the ones he had in his aquarium. This, though, was different. It was goldfish sized, but it had fabulous marbled-silvery markings, and a wonderful tail and fins that fanned out like exotic veils. Paul had never seen anything like it.

"Wow!" he said admiringly. "What sort of fish *is* it?"

"Blimey! I wouldn't even try to pronounce it, mate!" The stallholder cackled. "Very special, these are. Come on, try your luck!"

"Will it live in cold, fresh water?" Paul asked, thinking of his aquarium.

"Cold and fresh or hot and salty! Anything you like – these little beauties ain't fussy at all."

That was rubbish, and Paul was about to say so, but he didn't get the chance. "Twenty pee a go, son," the stallholder said. "Can't get cheaper than that, can you?"

You couldn't, Paul thought, and returned his grin. "OK, then." He plonked a coin into the man's hand.

The stallholder's mouth widened so enormously that for a moment Paul honestly thought his face would fall in half. "That's the way!" he said triumphantly. "Easy as pie, this game. You'll see!"

Paul didn't believe that for a moment. The man was here to make money, after all; the fish must have cost a lot more than twenty pence each, and if the game was that easy he'd soon be out of pocket.

"What do I do?" he asked.

He was handed five small, battered wooden

hoops. "Just get three of 'em over the pegs. Simple as that!"

There's a catch, Paul thought. *There's got to be.*

He was wrong. The hoops almost seemed to have a life of their own. Four of them dropped neatly over the pegs, and within less than a minute Paul found himself the surprised and delighted owner of one of the exotic-looking fish.

He held it up, staring at it. The fish stared back. It didn't goggle the way fish usually did. It looked more aware than that. As if it was studying him. Summing him up. *Thinking.*

"There you are, mate!" breezed the stall-holder. "He's all yours!"

Paul couldn't help noticing the odd way the man said the word *all*. He was still grinning, but there was a new glint in his eyes, and Paul wasn't entirely sure that he liked it.

"Take him home and pop him in a bowl, and he'll be happy as a cow in clover!" the man added. And he started to bellow out his patter again. "Win a fish! Win a luvly, lively little fish! Easy as pie, and only twenty pee a go!"

A very small boy going past with his mother

started to pester, "Mu-um! I-want-one-I-WANT-one!"

Behind them, Gemma signalled impatiently to Paul and mouthed, "Come on!"

Paul only went on staring at the fish, until his sister marched up to him and shook his arm.

"Come *on*, Paul! I've had enough of this dump; I'm bored. Let's go home."

The fish flipped its tail, almost as if it understood and agreed. Paul blinked, and came back to earth. For some reason there was suddenly a funny, twisty feeling in his stomach. With an effort he shook it off. Indigestion, probably. Gemma had warned him not to eat that second candy-floss. . .

The fish watched him. He smiled at it. Its tail waggled. "OK," said Paul, and followed Gemma across the fairground.

Paul had been interested in fish-keeping for four years, and had a good collection of goldfish, shubunkins and various other cold-water species. Arriving home, he took the new addition to his aquarium in the living room. Mum and Dad came in from the garden to see it, and

Bella, Paul and Gemma's four-year-old sister, trailed after them.

"New fish!" Bella exclaimed.

"Yes," said Paul. "And you leave it alone or else, all right?" Bella might look like an angel with her blonde hair and big blue eyes, but she certainly didn't behave like one. More than once Paul had caught her with her hand in the tank. And there had been that time when she'd almost succeeded in feeding two shubunkins to next door's cat. . . .

Bella scowled. "Don't like it anyway." She stuck her tongue out at the fish, but Paul ignored her as he emptied the plastic bag into the aquarium.

"It's certainly unusual," Dad said. "Not the kind you usually get at fairs. Will it be all right with the rest, Paul? They won't attack it or anything?"

"No, it'll be fine. Look." Paul pointed to where the new fish was already making itself at home. One or two of the others swam up to it, but after a vague look they drifted away again.

"Oh, well," said Dad. "If there aren't going to be any fireworks, I might as well go back to my weeding." He sounded disappointed, and

Gemma snorted with laughter.

"Huh!" Paul grunted disgustedly. Of course the fish weren't going to fight. The new arrival wouldn't cause any trouble – none at all.

Early the next morning, Paul lay in bed planning what he should do with the whole week of half-term that lay ahead. The weather was much better today, and if it stayed fine he and Gemma would probably spend most of their time on the beach at the Devon coastal town where they lived. With luck the sea would be just about warm enough for swimming.

He was in a good mood when he got up. But the mood vanished when he looked at his aquarium.

"Gem – two of my goldfish are missing."

"Uh?" Gemma looked up. She was rummaging through the pocket money she had left; she too was trying to plan out her week. "How do you know?"

"Because I can count, dumbo. There were seven of those small ones in here yesterday. Now there are only five."

"Bella's probably eaten them," said Gemma.

"Oh, ha ha." But the word *eaten* stuck in Paul's mind. The new fish was swimming quietly among the others. It didn't seem at all aggressive. And yet. . .

"Count them again," Gemma suggested. "They move around so fast, you probably got it wrong."

Paul tried it, then tried a third time. It made no difference; whatever he did, he couldn't change the total. There were definitely only five small fish.

Gemma raised her eyebrows. "I said you shouldn't have bothered with that hoop-la stall. You've probably gone and got yourself a piranha, or something!"

"Don't be so stupid!" But even as he said it Paul's stomach lurched with the same peculiar feeling he'd had yesterday. This time, it certainly wasn't indigestion.

"There's some other explanation," he added. "There must be."

"Like what?"

In truth Paul didn't know, but he didn't want to admit that to her. "Oh, loads of possibilities," he said airily. And he thought: *but I'll keep an eye on this fish. Just in case.*

* * *

Everything in the aquarium was fine that evening, when the two of them came back salty and sandy and cheerful from a day on the beach. But the following morning, Paul's biggest shubunkin had disappeared without trace.

It wasn't possible, Paul told himself. The shubunkin was as big as the new fish – surely the new one couldn't have eaten it? He stared through the glass of the tank, trying not to feel squeamish as he looked for some sign of remains. There was nothing.

Gemma came and peered over his shoulder. "The new one looks a bit bigger. . ." she said uneasily.

"That's just the glass distorting." Even as he said it, though, Paul wondered if she was right. The fish *did* seem to have grown slightly.

"I'll move it." He straightened up, shoving his fair hair out of his eyes in the way he always did when he felt nervous. "That old goldfish bowl's still in the cupboard. I'll put it in there, on its own. Then we'll soon see what's going on."

"If I were you, I'd get rid of it altogether," Gemma suggested darkly.

"Nah! you've been watching too many bad horror movies. It's only a fish."

"So was Jaws," said Gemma.

The fish settled happily into the bowl. It ate the food that Paul sprinkled for it and there was no more trouble in the aquarium. Paul went to bed that night convinced that he had solved the problem.

He was up early the next morning. Gemma was still in bed, Mum was having a shower, and Dad was making coffee that looked (and probably tasted) like old engine oil. Yawning, Paul went into the living room.

The first thing he saw was the goldfish bowl. It had water in it, but nothing else. The new fish had gone.

"What the—" Paul started to say. Then he stopped as he looked at the aquarium.

There was the new fish, drifting contentedly among all the rest.

Or rather, almost all the rest. Paul had had another shubunkin that he was especially proud of. It had different markings from the others, and it was tamer, too, often coming up to feed from his fingers. Yesterday, it had been there in the tank.

Today, it had vanished.

2

"I'll murder her!" Paul made another lunge with the net, only to see the fish wriggle away again. "This time I will, I really will *murder* her!"

Gemma yawned. She wasn't too pleased at having been hauled out of bed and dragged downstairs just because of this. "You don't know it was Bella," she pointed out reasonably.

"Oh, don't I? Who else could it have been?"

"Don't look at me!"

"Exactly. And it's hardly likely to have been Mum or Dad, either. So – oh, come *here*!"

There was a splashing, and the fish escaped again. "Look, get that other net, will you, and give me a hand?"

Hiding a grin, Gemma picked up the net. They managed to catch the fish at last, and put it back in the bowl. It stared at them through the glass, its fins waving gently. It didn't look any fatter. Or did it? Paul couldn't be sure. But it certainly didn't look as if it had eaten a whole shubunkin, and that put the seal on his suspicions.

"Right," he said ominously, shaking water from his hands. "Where's Bella?"

As if conjured up like a demon Bella appeared. She had been in the garden. Her hands were filthy, and there was grass in her hair.

"Come here, you little monster!" Paul pounced before Bella could dodge, and hauled her towards the tank. "You put the new fish back with the others!"

"Didn't!" Bella protested indignantly.

"Oh yes, you did! How many times have I told you not to touch them?"

"*Didn't!*" Bella repeated. "Stupid fish!" She blew a raspberry.

"Stupid me, more like, for thinking I can

leave you alone in here for one tenth of a second!" Paul retorted ferociously. "If you dare touch my fish again, if you go anywhere *near* them, then you will *die, very* slowly, and *very* horribly! Do you understand?"

Bella glared back defiantly. "Can't tell me what to do!"

"Oh yes I can, if you want to stay alive!"

"You're a big bully! I'll tell Mum!"

"Tell me what?" said a voice, and Mum appeared, with her hair wrapped in a towel. "Have you taken my hairdryer again, Gemma? I keep telling you—"

"Mum! Mum! Paul's being horrible to me!" Bella wailed.

"Well, that's nothing new." Mum looked at Paul. "What's she done this time?"

Paul told the story. To his dismay, though, Mum didn't take his side. He hadn't *seen* Bella move the fish, had he? Well then, how did anyone know it was her?

"It isn't fair to accuse someone without proof," Mum said, while Bella sheltered behind her and pulled faces. "Besides, the bowl's on a higher shelf than the tank. Bella couldn't even have reached it."

"See?" Bella added triumphantly. "Wasn't me!"

Paul opened his mouth to protest, then shut it again as he realized that Mum was right. Bella couldn't be the culprit – not unless she had climbed up the shelf unit.

Mind you, that was always a possibility. But it was no use saying so to Mum. Bella was cunning enough never to do her worst when their parents were around, so Mum and Dad didn't know the half of what she got up to. It looked as if she was going to get away with it this time, but if it happened again. . .

"All right," Paul said grumpily, "maybe it wasn't her. But—"

"Paul!" said Mum warningly. "Not without proof. All right?"

Paul sighed. "All right."

Mum went out, and Paul and Gemma glowered at Bella. She stared back pugnaciously, then demanded, "Say sorry!"

"Don't push it!" Paul snarled.

Bella smirked. Then, fast as a cat, she shot forward and wiped her grubby hands straight down the legs of Paul's clean jeans.

"Big pig!" she said, and fled before Paul

could grab her.

It took Paul half the morning to calm down. At last, though, he stopped seething enough to bike into the town centre and meet some of his friends. They cycled round the park, had a pizza, and then someone suggested the cinema. But Paul wasn't in the mood for that. He kept thinking about Bella's prank. And he kept thinking about the new fish.

He wished he had never won the wretched thing. The stallholder had talked him into it; he hadn't really wanted another one at all. And for all his jovial manner, the man had given him a distinct case of the creeps. Those howlingly loud clothes, and the way he grinned with his pointed teeth. . . He'd been evasive about the fish too, only saying it was "very special". There was something weird about all this, Paul thought, and he wanted to get to the bottom of it.

He didn't go to the cinema with the others. Instead, he went home and shut himself in his room. He had some books and magazines on fish keeping, and for the rest of the afternoon he trawled through them, looking for something – anything, in fact – about the strange new fish.

He found nothing – not a picture, not a single word. Whatever the fish was, it didn't figure in any of these papers. "Very special", all right, he thought. So special that none of the experts seemed to have heard of it.

He gave up his search at tea-time, and after tea went back upstairs to play computer games. He could hear Gemma's TV from her room next door, and along the landing Bella was shouting and singing at the top of her voice as Mum bathed her. At least the brat would be in bed soon, Paul thought sourly, and he could have some peace and quiet downstairs.

Just as he thought the words "peace and quiet", Bella's singing changed. From a hideously awful rendition of the "Neighbours" theme, her voice suddenly shot up the scale to a note that would have made an operatic soprano jealous. Paul was so startled that for a moment he didn't realize what was happening – but then it dawned on him. Bella wasn't singing. She was *screaming*.

For all his fury with his little sister, blood was

still thicker than water, and Paul raced from his room. On the landing he collided with Gemma, who said, "What on earth—"

"I don't know! Come on!"

They ran to the bathroom and burst in. Mum had whisked Bella out of the bath, and Bella, still shrieking, was clinging to her like a wriggling pink lobster.

And the bath water was churning agitatedly.

"Fish!" Bella yelled. "Fish!"

Paul and Gemma stared in astonishment. "Mum, what's going on? What's the matter with her?"

"I don't know!" Mum told them. "One moment she was all right, then she suddenly started screaming." She hugged the little girl. "Bella! Bella, what's the matter?"

"*Fish!*" Bella howled. "It bited me! On my toe!"

"What?" Mum looked at Bella's kicking foot, but there was nothing there. Puzzled, she then turned to look at Paul and Gemma. They gazed blankly back at her, and Gemma said, "I don't understand!"

But Paul thought he did. He swung round and dropped to a crouch beside the bath. The water wasn't churning any more, but under the foam of Bella's bubble-bath, he glimpsed a small, sleek shape. Moving. Swimming.

Gemma, peering, said in astonishment, "It's—"

"Don't tell me," Paul interrupted. "I can see it for myself."

"But how—"

"I don't *know*, all right? I haven't got the foggiest idea!"

It was crazy. It was insane. In fact, it couldn't possibly have happened. But his fish – his new, mysterious fish – had somehow got into Bella's bath. And if Bella was telling the truth for once, it had *nipped* her.

He pushed aside a froth of bubbles. Under the water, the fish stared up at him. Its tail waggled, as if it was pleased with itself.

"Gemma," Paul said through clenched teeth, "get the net. . ."

3

Mum came down to the living-room, shut the door and said, "All right. Just what did you two think you were doing?"

Paul and Gemma looked up in surprise from the bowl, where they had replaced the fish. Paul started to say, "What do you mean?" but he wasn't allowed to finish.

"I suppose you thought it was fair game, did you? A way of paying Bella back for what you accused her of doing this morning?"

"You don't think I—" Paul said.

"Oh, I don't just *think* it, my lad! It's obvious! You deliberately put that fish in Bella's bath, to scare her!"

"But I didn't!" Paul protested. "Honestly, Mum, I've no idea how it got there!"

"I think Bella did it herself," Gemma put in, defending Paul.

Mum glared at her. "Do you? Well, I'd like to know how, as she wasn't out of my sight once I started the bath running!"

Paul and Gemma looked at each other in dismay. While they were going through the whole rigmarole of catching the fish and putting it back, they had worked out how Bella must have done it or thought they had. Now, though. . .

"Where is Bella?" Gemma asked.

"In bed. She's calmed down, and Dad's reading her a story."

"It didn't really bite her, did it?"

"No, but that's no thanks to either of you. I'm especially angry with you, Paul. I thought you might have grown out of such silly and spiteful tricks at your age!"

Paul tried to explain, tried to make Mum believe that he was innocent, but it was useless. Who else could have put the fish in the bath? Mum said. It was no use Paul pointing out that this very morning Mum had lectured him about not accusing people without proof – she only told him not to be so cheeky, and wouldn't listen. Paul – and probably Gemma, too – *had* to be guilty.

Paul and Gemma, though, knew the truth, and Mum's disbelief couldn't make any difference. When she finally finished hauling them over the coals, they escaped to Paul's room and flopped down on the bed. For a minute they were silent. Then Gemma said, "Right. So how *did* it get there?"

Paul sighed. "Search me, Gem. It's weird. Almost as if it . . . did it by itself." He laughed to show that he wasn't being serious, but the laughter was forced.

Gemma wrinkled her nose. "Jumped out of the bowl, flapped upstairs and into the bath, you mean? Well, I've heard of flying fish, but. . ."

Her attempt at a joke fell flat, and for another minute they both sat staring gloomily at the carpet. At last Gemma ventured, "How about putting a lid on the bowl?"

"It'd suffocate. Fish have to have oxygen."

"Well, a mesh or something, then."

Paul looked at his sister uneasily. "You're talking as if you think it *did* get out by itself."

"I know," Gemma said. "And that's crazy, isn't it? The only snag is. . ."

Her voice trailed off and Paul prompted, "What?"

Gemma chewed her lower lip. "The only snag is . . . I just can't think of any other possible explanation."

Paul couldn't sleep that night. Long after his parents were in bed he was still awake, staring through his window at the moon, as a battle went on in his mind.

A small voice inside him was telling him that he had to do something about the fish. It wouldn't be enough just to put a mesh over the bowl, as Gemma had suggested – the voice was warning him to get rid of it altogether. This left him with two choices: he could give it to someone else, or he could kill it.

Killing it, of course, was out of the question. Paul simply couldn't do it; squeamishness aside, it wasn't fair to the fish. It hadn't actually *harmed* anyone (well, only Bella, and only a bit, and it served her right anyway). And if it *had* eaten the others in the aquarium, that was Paul's own fault for putting it in there. It was just a fish. It was only doing what was natural to it, and it couldn't help its nature. No, he couldn't get rid of it like that.

So, how about giving it away? But Paul's conscience squirmed again. Even if it was "just a fish", he couldn't ignore the fact that some very strange things had happened since he had brought it home. Again, it didn't seem fair to offer it to one of his friends without telling them the whole story. If he did that, they would think he was insane, and they certainly wouldn't want the fish.

Paul sighed. It was beginning to look as if Gemma's suggestion was the best after all, though the thought that the fish could have got out of the bowl by itself . . . well, it was mad enough to make anyone howl with laughter.

So why didn't he feel like laughing?

He turned his head and looked thoughtfully at the bedroom door. If he went downstairs now, in the dead of night, what would he find in the living room? Was the fish still safely in its bowl or had it, *could* it have, moved again?

Though Paul felt he ought to find out, he didn't have the nerve. There were too many "what ifs" in his mind; his imagination was working overtime. In fact (though he'd never have admitted it to anyone but himself), he was getting very nervous about the whole thing.

Don't be a scaredy-cat, part of him said, using a favourite expression of Bella's. *Go and look.* But his cowardly self argued, *No, leave it till morning.*

His cowardly self won, as he knew it would. Paul turned over in bed, buried his head under the duvet, and willed himself to go to sleep and forget all about fish of any kind.

4

Paul hurled himself through the kitchen door, and his fingers scrabbled for the light switch. Nothing happened when he pressed it. Everything stayed pitch dark. And *it* was coming down the hall, lurching and flopping, coming after him. . .

"*Aarghh!*" Paul let out a yell as something enormously heavy crashed against the door. It burst open – and there was the fish, big as a shark now, barrelling towards him and using its fins like hands. Its ferocious teeth snapped and clashed at his heels, and with another yell he twisted round, leaped past it as it lunged at him, and raced back along the hall again.

"*Dad! Mum! Gem!*" he screamed. No one answered him. There was no one else here – only him, and the monstrous fish. He could hear it coming after him again and he struggled to open the front door. But it was stuck fast, and none of the lights would work, and he was trapped in the house, in the dark, with a horror that pursued him relentlessly.

He sprang for the stairs as the fish appeared again from the kitchen. It was glowing with a horrible greenish light, and as it flopped along it made a wet, bubbling noise that almost sounded like words.

"*TRY YOUR LUCK ... TRY YOUR LUCK!*" The fish had a tweed hat on its head, and the bubbling noise *had* become words now. The stairs seemed to have turned to soft toffee; Paul's feet stuck as he tried to climb them, and his hands slipped on the banisters as if they were made of ice.

Bubbling and flopping, the fish reached the bottom of the stairs. It leered up at him and its teeth gnashed so fast that they were a blur. Then it started to slither up towards him.

"No!" Paul shouted. "You can't live out of water! You can't!"

The fish laughed at him. *"EASY AS PIE, EASY AS PIE!"* bubbled the hideous voice. *"ONLY TWENTY PEE A GO!"* Its body was swelling to an even greater size, pushing the banisters outwards with a crack of splintering wood. Its mouth opened wider, wider, turning into a vast black cavern filled with deadly knives. . .

With a yell of terror Paul woke up and shot bolt upright in bed, heart thundering with shock.

The room was filled with daylight, but it was several seconds before he could make himself believe that the hideous dream hadn't been real. When he did finally convince himself, he breathed a gigantic sigh of sheer relief. Then, not wanting to go back to sleep and risk another nightmare, he scrambled out of bed. It wasn't until he was half dressed that he realized it was only six o'clock, but what the heck? It wouldn't hurt him to get up early for once. It looked as if the weather was going to be good. Maybe he would go to the beach. It would help him to forget the dream.

Feeling better, he finished dressing and went downstairs, tiptoeing so that he wouldn't disturb anyone. Even Bella wasn't awake yet. *Makes a change,* Paul thought. Usually, Bella was up and thundering around like a herd of elephants long before the rest of the family.

At the bottom of the stairs, he reached for the living-room door-handle. Then paused as he remembered what had happened late last night. He had wanted to go down and take a look at the fish . . . but he had been scared of what he might find. Now, with the awful dream fresh in his mind, he suddenly had the same uneasy feeling. What *would* he find in that room? Everything normal? Or. . .

His pulse started to speed up again, and it made him angry with himself. What on earth was the matter with him? Anyone would think the fish was lurking behind the door, waiting to attack, the way it had done in his nightmare. . .

"Oh, stop being such an idiot!" Paul said aloud. He grabbed the door-handle, twisted it and strode into the room.

His heart gave an enormous lurch as he went in. It was only a reflex, but with the curtains closed the room looked ominous, almost threatening. Paul hurried to the window and hacked the curtains back. Light flooded in, and he let out his pent-up breath, telling himself he was being totally stupid.

Then he turned to the aquarium and bowl.

The aquarium looked fine, the goldfish and shubunkins swimming peacefully around. Paul didn't stop to count them, but there were no signs of trouble. Relieved, he looked up to the higher shelf, where the bowl stood.

The new fish wasn't there.

Paul's jaw dropped. He stared at the bowl until the truth sank in, then scrambled back to the aquarium, expecting to see the fish goggling – or more likely smirking – at him through the glass. But there was no sign of it, and after a disbelieving minute Paul stepped back and tried to think.

Where had the fish gone? Bella couldn't be blamed this time; she had been in bed and asleep long before Paul took a final look at the bowl last night. Gemma wouldn't have moved it without telling him. Mum? She had been pretty furious about the incident in the bathroom, but she surely wouldn't get rid of the fish?

31

Could it have jumped out of the bowl? Paul started to search the floor around the shelves, half expecting to find the fish's corpse on the carpet. But there was nothing, and at last he straightened up, baffled and defeated.

It seemed horribly likely that the fish was dead. Maybe it had died in the bowl, last night after he was in bed. If it had, his parents might have taken it out. Or maybe Sammy, next door's cat, had got into the house. Sammy was very fond of fish.

He felt a pang of pity for the fish. Despite the trouble it had caused, it hadn't deserved to die. If Mum or Dad had got rid of it, chances were that it would be in the rubbish bin. That didn't seem right somehow. At very least, it should have a decent burial in the garden.

With a sigh, Paul headed for the kitchen to find some rubber gloves and start searching.

Paul was still rummaging when Bella pounded downstairs a little while later. She stared at the mess her brother had made and said, "Mum'll kill you."

Paul jumped, startled, and cracked his head on the edge of the worktop. "Don't creep up on me like that!" he said savagely, rubbing his skull.

"Didn't," retorted Bella. "I made loads of noise. What're you doing?"

"Looking for buried treasure, what else?"

"Pooey!" Bella said scornfully. It was her favourite word at the moment. Then, "Where's that nasty fish gone?"

Well, that told him something, Paul thought. Bella might be crafty, but she wasn't clever enough to pretend she didn't know where the fish was if she did.

"I don't know," he admitted sourly. "It's disappeared. I'm hunting for it."

"In there? Fishes don't go in there!"

"I know they don't! But if you've got a better idea, I'd like to hear it!"

Bella considered this. "I'll look, too," she announced at last. Then her eyes lit up evilly. "If I find it, I'll give it to Sammy."

She shot out of the door before Paul could tell her what he thought of her.

Paul, Bella and, later, Gemma, found no trace of the missing fish. As Bella had predicted, Mum was far from pleased when she came downstairs and saw the contents of the kitchen rubbish bin all over the floor. When Paul explained, she said exasperatedly, "Well, it's nothing to do with me or Dad. We didn't touch the wretched thing. I expect Sammy got in somehow and ate it, and quite honestly, it's good riddance as far as I'm concerned. I can't imagine why you had to have another fish in the first place; you've already got so many. Now I want a cup of tea, so clear that mess up and get out from under my feet!"

Defeated, Paul cleared up, then went dejectedly out into the garden. Gemma followed him.

"Mum's right in a way, Paul," she said. "That fish has been nothing but a nuisance since the minute you got it."

"That's not the point," Paul told her. "I want to know what *happened* to it! How the heck did it get out of the bowl?"

"Like Mum said, maybe Sammy—"

"Oh, come on! I wondered that at first, but it's impossible. You know how paranoid Dad is; he goes round locking the house up like a fortress every night. An ant couldn't have got in, let alone a cat!" He paused. "And how did it get back into the aquarium, that first time? Or into Bella's bath?"

Gemma was forced to admit that she didn't have a sensible answer. "Well, one way or another it's vanished now," she said. Then she looked sidelong at her brother and added cautiously, "Like Mum said, it's probably good riddance."

She expected Paul to flare up at her, and he nearly did. But common sense stopped him. The fish *had* been a nuisance. And there *was* something very weird about it. Deep down, he was glad it had gone.

He sighed and said, "Yeah. Maybe it is."

The trouble was, Paul thought later, the fish was bugging him. Because no matter how hard he thought, and turned the facts upside-down and inside-out in his mind, he could *not* work out what had happened to it.

He did search in a few more places. The most obvious was the garden pond. Quite a few gardens in their street had ponds, and until recently most had contained large goldfish. Then a heron had discovered the ponds, and now no one had any fish left. All the same,

Paul thought it was worth a look. But after half an hour of poking around among the water-plants, he gave up. It was daft, anyway. The missing fish couldn't possibly have jumped out of the bowl and flopped all the way to the pond.

Any more than it could have flopped to the bathroom, said a small inner voice. Paul shivered, and pushed the voice away.

Then, from the kitchen, came a startled shriek.

"Mum?" Paul jumped to his feet and ran indoors. Mum was standing in front of the sink, looking at a bowl of soapy washing-up water. She was sucking two of her fingers, and as Paul appeared in the doorway she pointed at the bowl with her other hand and yelled, "I suppose you think that's funny!"

"What?" Paul started forward and peered at the bowl. Rims of breakfast plates protruded out of the water like colourful icebergs, but there was something else there – something that wasn't a plate or a cup or a spoon, or any-thing else that ought to be in a bowl of washing-up.

"It *bit* me!" Mum raged. "Look at this!" She

held out her fingers. There was a bead of blood on one of them.

The fish could see them both, Paul was certain of it. It was watching them, almost as if it was enjoying the joke.

But this didn't feel like a joke any more.

5

"It *is* bigger," Gemma said uneasily. "In fact, I'd say it's grown about three centimetres since yesterday."

Paul didn't answer. He dared not, because he agreed with her and didn't want to acknowledge it. The fish gazed back through the glass and fanned its tail and fins lazily. They had both been trying to outstare it, but had found they couldn't; the fish had a patience and determination that was unnerving, and it simply wouldn't look away. Paul thought: *It's challenging us. It knows we're getting the wind up, and it's enjoying every moment.*

What sort of creature have I landed myself with?

"You've got to decide what to do with it now," Gemma told him. "You know what Mum said — she won't have it in the house any longer." She paused. "I think you should get rid of it altogether. Kill it, if you have to."

Paul squirmed inwardly. "I can't do that," he said. "Not in cold blood."

"You don't mind the fish you *eat* being killed. What's the difference?"

"You do it, then." She wouldn't, he knew; she was much more squeamish than he was.

Gemma looked uncomfortable. "Well . . . dump it somewhere. Why not take it down to the beach and let it go in the sea?"

It was a thought . . . but it gave Paul a better idea.

"Why don't we put it in the pond?" he suggested.

"That heron still comes round. He'd—" Then Gemma stopped and a grin spread slowly over her face. "Oh, right, I get it. You can't bring yourself to kill the fish, but if the heron does it for you, that's all right." She shrugged. "Sounds fair enough to me. And if the heron doesn't get it, it'll probably eat the pond snails Mum's always grumbling about. That'll put you in her good books."

"Something's got to!" Paul said with feeling.

Mum was still convinced that the whole thing had been a practical joke, like Bella and the bath. Paul couldn't blame her. After all, if he couldn't come up with a better explanation, what else could she be expected to believe?

They carried the fish in its bowl out to the garden, and tipped it carefully into the pond. Gemma looked up at the clear blue sky and called, "Hey, heron! Lunch!"

"Oh, shut up!" Paul watched the fish swim away and hide under a water-lily leaf. He felt guilty and relieved at the same time, and the mixture was confusing him. But at least he had got the fish out of the house without having to kill it himself. It had a chance in the pond. And, apart from giving it some food now and then, with a bit of luck he could forget about it.

The fish didn't need to be given any food. By teatime that day every snail in the pond had vanished, together with a large clump of frogspawn that had been under one of the plants. Bella had been avidly watching the frogspawn for weeks, waiting for it to hatch. Convinced that the frogs she would eventually have would be poisonous, she had planned to cause havoc with them, and she was livid to find the spawn gone.

But if Bella was furious, Mum was delighted to have the pond cleared. The snails were gone, and Paul's strange fish was out of sight and out of mind at the far end of the garden. Everyone was happy.

Until the next morning.

It was Gemma who found the grisly remains at the side of the pond. A heap of grey feathers, two clawed feet, and a long beak. Plus a brownish-red smear on the paving, leading to the water's edge. It looked very, very much like dried blood.

Gemma stared at the mess for a long time, trying to tell herself that the remains were not what she thought they were. But there couldn't be any doubt: she had seen the heron too often to make a mistake.

Using a lot of elaborate sign language she managed to get Paul outside without alerting their parents. There was a long, unpleasant silence as they stood by the pond together. Then at last Paul raised his head.

"It could have been Sammy. . ." he said nervously. There was an answering mew, and at the sound of his name Sammy appeared from next-door's garden hedge. They looked at him. He was only a small cat, and the heron had been a big bird. He couldn't have eaten it – he just *couldn't*!

Sammy blinked at them, then disappeared back into the hedge. "That's weird," said Gemma. "He usually comes to be stroked."

"I know. But he doesn't seem too keen this morning, does he? It's as if he's. . ." Paul didn't want to voice what he was thinking, so Gemma made herself say it for him.

"Scared."

"Yeah."

Then they both spoke at the same time. Paul began, "So if something—", while Gemma started, "What could have—" and they stopped. There wasn't any point asking the question.

Slowly, uneasily, their gazes met.

"I think we should move . . . this . . . somewhere Mum and Dad won't find it," Paul

42

suggested, nodding at the remains of the heron.

Gemma shivered. "All right. Then what?"

Paul chewed his lower lip. This time, something *must* be done. Something drastic. The fish, quite simply, had to go.

"Let's talk when we've cleared up," he said. An unpleasant thought came to him. "Though of course we'll have to catch it first. . ."

"I don't want to think about that," said Gemma. "Not until I have to."

Trying not to be sick, they shovelled the bits of dead heron into a plastic bin-bag, which they hid behind the garden shed. Bella, luckily, had been taken to a friend's house to play, so she wasn't around to poke her nose in and ask awkward questions as, armed with nets and sticks, they returned to the pond. Gemma pulled floating clumps of water-weed aside, and Paul searched for the fish. But he couldn't find it. The pond appeared to be completely empty.

"You don't think it could be. . ." Gemma ventured.

Paul's eyes widened. "Back in the aquarium?

Oh, no – it can't be, surely!" He jumped to his feet and ran indoors to look.

Gemma went on hunting until he came back, and she didn't know whether to be relieved or dismayed when he said, "It's not there, or in the bowl."

"No goldfish missing?"

"No. I counted. It *must* be in here, Gem. We'd better keep looking."

But they still hadn't found it when Mum came out and told them to stop messing around. They were both supposed to help with chores in the school holidays, but this morning, as Mum crossly put it, they hadn't lifted a finger between them.

"Your rooms look like Woolworths after the H-Bomb!" she lectured. "And it's Paul's turn to hoover, and someone's left a great tide-mark in the bath, and I want some shopping done."

She was feeling grumpy this morning, and Paul and Gemma knew better than to argue or try to wriggle out. Exchanging a look that said silently, *We'll try again later*, they resigned themselves to a boring hour of housework.

They tossed up for who would do what; Gemma won and went thankfully off to the shops with Mum's list, while Paul, feeling like a martyr, tramped upstairs to tackle the bath. He got it clean (well, clean enough; who cared about a few marks here and there), then decided to reward himself with some orange squash before getting on with the hoovering.

"What's for dinner tonight, Mum?" he asked as he went into the kitchen.

"Pork chops." Mum was unloading the wash-ing-machine; her voice sounded hollow as she stuck her head half-inside it, looking for a miss-ing sock. "They're defrosting in the fridge."

"Great!" Pork chops were one of Paul's favourites, and as Gemma and Bella had both gone off them since seeing *Babe*, that meant all the more for him. He opened the fridge door. "What about afters?"

"Good grief! Don't you ever think about any-thing except food?" Mum said. "If you really want to know, I've just made a raspberry jelly. It's still liquid, so mind you don't knock it flying if you're rummaging in there."

She went outside with the wet washing. Paul grinned, reaching for the squash bottle. As his fingers closed round it, he saw an empty plate in the fridge. Odd. . .Whatever was it doing there? Then suddenly his grin broke into a laugh as he realized that Mum must have put it there for the pork chops, then forgotten to take the chops themselves out of the freezer.

"You're getting absent-minded in your old age, Mum!" Paul said aloud. Luckily for him Mum was too far away down the garden to hear the comment, and Paul's grin broke into a laugh. He'd get the chops out, save her the bother – *and* he could choose the biggest ones while he was at it.

He reached towards the freezer . . . and stopped. The fridge door was still open, and he had suddenly noticed something. The plate wasn't entirely empty. There were a few scraps on it. *Meaty* scraps. And some traces of ice.

On the shelf below, a slight movement caught Paul's eye. He looked . . . and his pulse slowed to a thick, pumping crawl.

The jelly that Mum had made was in a large glass bowl on the shelf. It had been covered with cling film, but the cling film had a gaping hole in it. Bubbles were rising slowly, steadily to the top of the jelly's liquid surface. And under the surface was an all too familiar shape.

The fish positively *leered* at Paul through the

curved glass of the bowl. It was most definitely, certainly, undoubtedly bigger; and as Paul gaped back at it, it opened its mouth and emitted a new stream of bubbles, like a huge, silent burp.

Which, after five pork chops, wasn't the least bit surprising.

Paul didn't know how he managed to do all he did in the few minutes it took Mum to hang out the washing. Later he could hardly even *remember* doing it; he was on a kind of auto-pilot of sheer panic. Out with the bowl, dump it on the draining-board, snatch an empty jar from the cupboard. Trying to grab a fish that flapped and wriggled and was slippery with liquid jelly was a superhuman task, but at last, somehow, he managed it.

As he lifted the fish out of the jelly, it bit him.

"*Oww!*" The pain in his finger was so sharp that Paul almost let the fish go again – which was, of course, exactly what it had intended. It flipped up in the air, Paul made a despairing grab and, to his surprise and relief, his hands closed round its writhing body before it could get away. Off-balance, he shoved it towards the jar. It flopped in – and Paul's elbow knocked the jelly bowl. He saw it happening but couldn't stop it. The bowl skidded off the drainer, and smashed on the floor in an explosion of glass and raspberry goo.

Mum came in to find Paul picking glass shards from the floor. She stopped in the doorway and said, "Oh, *Paul*!"

Paul looked up guiltily. "I knocked it. Sorry, Mum."

He braced himself for a lecture of the "didn't-I-tell-you-to-be-careful-and-why-don't-you-ever-listen" variety. But Mum didn't know the whole story. She didn't realize that the pork chops defrosting in the fridge had only just been taken out of the freezer. And she didn't notice the jar, with its lid tightly in place, that stood on the draining board – which was just as well. Because every few seconds the jar gave an angry little jiggle, as though something inside it was trying very hard indeed to get out.

6

Coming home with the shopping, Gemma almost jumped out of her skin when Paul pounced on her from behind the front door.

"Aargh!" she shrieked. "Paul, what do you think you're—"

"Shh!" Paul waved his hands frantically. "Keep your voice down!"

Sometimes Gemma could be very slow on the uptake, because she started to say loudly, "Why? What are you doing, lurking and scaring me like that?"

"Gem, please! I don't want Mum to hear!" Paul flung a nervous glance towards the kitchen. "Dump the shopping, and come up to my room. It's *urgent*."

She got the message at last, and hurried upstairs a few minutes later. Paul was pacing his bedroom like a caged tiger; seeing her, he hissed, "Shut the door!"

"All right, all right! What's the fuss? And why all this MI6 stuff?"

He told her. Gemma listened, her eyes growing wider and wider, and when the story was finished she let out a long whistle. "That isn't just weird," she said. "It's dead scary!"

"Tell me about it!" Paul agreed feelingly. "Look, Gem, it's no good. We've got to get rid of that fish once and for all."

"*We?*" Gemma raised her eyebrows. "I said that ages ago, if you remember."

"OK, so you were right; don't rub it in. What I thought was, if we took it to the beach, we could put it in the sea, or into a rock pool." He glanced uneasily round the room, as if half expecting the fish to jump out from a corner and shout *Boo*!

Gemma looked self-righteous. "I said that, too. *If* you—"

"Remember, yes, all *right*. Give me a break!"

Satisfied that she had made her point, Gemma said, "You want me to come with you, is that it?"

"Yes." Paul didn't like admitting that the fish spooked him so badly now that he didn't want to be alone with it for a single second, so he added, "I want a witness. To make sure it really does go."

"Suits me. I'll be as glad to see the back of it as you will." Gemma stood up. "Come on, then. The sooner we do it, the better we'll feel. Where is it now?"

"Back in the goldfish bowl downstairs."

"Fine. We'd better not take it in that, though. We'll find something that isn't glass, so no one will see it. Let's go."

Paul half expected the fish to have gone from the bowl when they went down to the living room. But, to his relief, it was still there. Mind you, he thought, with a plate over the bowl, and a heavy paperweight *and* two thumping great stones from the garden on top of that, it would need to be a Stallone of the fish world to get out.

Though how it had done a lot of other

things, including getting into the fridge, was a question he didn't want to think about.

They emptied the bowl, fish and all, into Bella's beach bucket, which was garish red and yellow plastic and had a snap-on lid. Mum was upstairs now, so they managed to reach the front door without being seen. When they opened it, though, their spirits sank.

Bella was stumping up the path, having just been brought home by her friend's mother. She took one look at what they were carrying and demanded indignantly, "Where are you going with my bucket?"

Paul opened his mouth to say, "Never you mind," which would have been a big mistake with Bella. But Gemma came to the rescue.

"Mum's got a present for you," she said in a conspiratorial voice.

Bella forgot the bucket instantly. "Present? What is it?"

"I'm not allowed to tell. It's a surprise. It's in the garden."

Bella's eyes lit up greedily. She didn't say another word but pushed past them and pelted through the door and along the hall.

"That's fixed her!" Gemma said with satisfaction.

"By the time she finds out there isn't a present, we'll be out of sight."

"Mum'll have our guts for winding her up," Paul pointed out.

"I know. But it's worth it." Gemma chuckled. "Pity we can't hang around and see Bella's face!"

But that was out of the question, so they set off at a fast walk down the long hill that led to the beach.

The beach was past the harbour and round the headland from where the local river ran into the sea. As it was Bank Holiday week there were quite a lot of people around, and Gemma frowned at the array of spread towels, sunshades, paddlers and bathers.

"We'd better not do it here," she said. "Let's go through the tunnel."

Strictly speaking there were two beaches here, separated by a cliff outcrop. You could climb across the boulders from one to the other at low tide, but otherwise the only way to reach the second beach was via a tunnel in the cliff. The Smugglers' Tunnel, it was called, though everyone knew that was just a name cooked up for the tourists. Paul and Gemma trudged up the slope to the tunnel entrance, and hurried through the dank, echoey passage. They emerged at the top of a flight of steps, and surveyed the sand below them.

"Quieter," Paul said, "but still enough people around to make things difficult. We'd better go right to the far end. There's that big pool; you know the one, just near where the beach ends. We'll dump the fish in there."

Kicking off their shoes as they reached the sand, they ploughed along the shore. The sea glittered in the sun, and the sails of small boats looked like colourful sharks' fins, which Paul certainly didn't want to be reminded of. At the far end of the beach, it was much quieter. The only other people anywhere nearby were a father, mother and three small children, who were exploring among the rocks. They had a little terrier dog that tore about in circles and barked excitedly, but neither the dog nor its owners took any notice of Paul and Gemma.

Paul pointed to where a knee of rock protruded from the cliffs. "There's the pool."

"Right." Gemma was taking a turn at carrying the bucket. It was starting to feel unnaturally heavy, and she would be glad to put it down.

The pool began at the knee of rock, and extended back into a wide, low cave. There were smaller rocks and clumps of seaweed in the pool – a perfect fish habitat – and though it was shallow at the edges, it became deeper in the cave, where shadows turned the water a dark and ominous-looking green, with strange reflections stirring in it.

They stopped on the brink of the pool, and Gemma gave a sigh as she let the bucket drop to the sand.

"Whew! Anyone would think it was full of stones!"

"I thought that, too," said Paul. He looked at the bucket. "There aren't any air-holes in the lid. For all we know, the fish might have. . ."

"Died?" Gemma finished for him. A tinge of hope had crept into her voice: it was an unkind thought, of course, but it *would* solve a lot of problems.

As if the fish had heard her, the bucket gave a lurch and from inside came the sound of water sloshing. Gemma looked disappointed and guilty in equal measure, and Paul sighed.

"Oh, well! Come on, then; let's get rid of it."

Gemma glanced over her shoulder as her

brother heaved the bucket to the pool's edge. "Those people with the dog are heading this way."

Paul looked. "Never mind. They can't see what we're doing, and even if they could, so what?" All the same, he had a sudden feeling that he wanted to hurry; to get the fish out of the bucket and walk away from it as quickly as possible. He wrestled with the lid, which seemed to be stuck.

"Put the whole bucket under the water," Gemma suggested.

"OK." Paul waded into the pool with Gemma following. They dunked the bucket in. Bubbles came from beneath the lid, but it still refused to come off. Then they heard barking.

Gemma said, "Oh, blast!" and waded out of the water. As she emerged, with a lot of splashing, the little terrier came bounding up to her with its stumpy tail wagging madly. It barked, jumped high in the air, then dropped to a crouch and barked again.

"Go away!" Gemma flapped her hands at the dog. "Go *away!*"

"He wants you to play with him," Paul

said. "Throw a stick or something."

"Where do you expect me to find a stick round here?"

"Well, a bit of seaweed, then, or a pebble – anything! Just get rid of him!"

Gemma snatched up a smooth pebble and hurled it as far as she could towards the sea. Barking ecstatically, the terrier shot off in pursuit with its tail going like a propellor.

"Quick!" Gemma said to Paul. "Before it comes back!"

Paul wrenched at the bucket lid again – and abruptly it came free. For one awful moment as he looked into the bucket he thought the fish wasn't there. But then he saw it, lurking at the bottom. It waved its fins. It sneered at him.

"Get out!" Paul told it through clenched teeth. "Go on, go away! I never want to see you again!"

The fish's tail flipped carelessly. It gave him one last look, then darted out of the bucket and arrowed away into the dark depths of the pool.

Remembering his finger, and Mum's, Paul scrambled out of the water as fast as he could. Back on dry land, he emptied the water out of the bucket and stared at the pool. The surface was smooth. There was no sign of the fish.

Gemma looked towards the sea and said, "That dog's coming back."

"Well, there's no need for us to hang around any more. Let's get going before it starts pestering us."

The dog, though, didn't follow them as they hurried away. Its owners called, "Dinky! Here, Dinky!" (which made Paul smother a snort of laughter) and it veered off to play with them instead. Paul and Gemma could hear it barking as they headed back the way they had come.

When they were well clear, Gemma looked round. The family had reached the pool, but she could hear the children's father telling them not to paddle in it because it was too deep. They obeyed.

But the dog didn't.

"Oh, no. . ." said Gemma.

Paul looked, and stopped dead. The terrier had plunged straight into the pool, and was swimming around blissfully. The three children laughed, jumping up and down on the edge and shouting, "Go on, Dinky! Go on!"

It was all so horribly inevitable that Paul and Gemma could only stand frozen and staring.

The terrier swam in circles, just the way it had run around on the sand. It was still barking. The children were encouraging it.

Then suddenly there was a new splashing. The dog's barks changed to a high-pitched snarl, and there was a terrific commotion in the water.

"Dinky!" the children's voices became shrill with alarm. "Dinky, *Dinky!*"

Dinky was thrashing in the pool, and now the snarling gave way to terrified yelps. The children started to scream, and their father was shouting, wading into the water in an effort to grab the dog and haul it out.

Amid all the din Paul and Gemma stared towards the pool. Their faces were white. Gemma opened her mouth as if to say something, but shut it again.

She looked at Paul. Paul looked at her.

Without a word they turned and pelted away along the beach as fast as they could run.

7

They didn't speak as they walked home. Paul was racked with guilt, and he suspected Gemma felt much the same. But he couldn't bring himself to say anything about it. In fact he couldn't bring himself to say anything at all.

He thought a lot, though. For a while he tried to tell himself that maybe things weren't as bad as they had looked. It was possible that the terrier simply couldn't swim very well, got into difficulty and was only yelping to be rescued. Perhaps it was now perfectly safe and well, with nothing more than a telling-off to show for its adventure.

But the idea wasn't very convincing, and with another stab of guilt Paul pushed his theory away. He felt awful, and even the thought that the fish wasn't his problem any more didn't help much.

Bella was waiting for them when they reached their house. Her face was like thunder and her fists were clenched as she called them Big Pigs and Smelly Stinkies and a few worse things besides. Mum, too, was hopping mad; not so much because they had deceived Bella, but because Bella had made such a nuisance of herself demanding her non-existent "present". But even she couldn't help noticing the way Paul and Gemma accepted the lecture she gave them. It wasn't that they didn't listen; it was as though they had something else on their minds, something that worried them.

However, Mum's efforts to find out what was wrong met with a blank wall, and at last she gave up. Paul went upstairs, looking like someone who, as Dad would have put it, had lost a ten-pound note and found a penny, while Gemma trailed disconsolately into the living-room. Mum watched them both go, then sighed and went to the kitchen to see how the pork chops were coming along.

Paul had only been in his room for a minute when a pounding of feet announced Gemma. She burst in without knocking, but before he could object, the look on her face stopped him.

She said: "Paul, I think you'd better come downstairs. Now."

She wouldn't explain as he followed her along the landing and down to the hall. The living room door was open. Gemma stood back to let him go in first. When he did, he couldn't work out at first what had got his sister so agitated.

Then he looked at his aquarium.

All his goldfish and shubunkins were gone. In their place, staring through the tank's glass side with a look of smug satisfaction, was *that* fish.

Paul's eyes bulged as he tried to take in the truth. Very slowly he backed away, until he collided with Gemma, who had followed him into the room. In a small, quavering voice he asked, "How. . .?"

"Your guess," said Gemma grimly, "is as good as mine."

The fish flipped its tail and turned its back on

them, as if they were beneath its notice. A part of Paul's whirling mind registered the fact that it was bigger than a mackerel now. Must be thirty centimetres at least – though he had no intention of getting close enough to it to check.

Pushing Gemma before him, he withdrew from the room and, very quietly, shut the door.

"I don't think Mum can have seen it yet," Gemma said. She was whispering, as if afraid that the fish would overhear and understand. Which, Paul thought with an inward shudder, it just might. "We ought to move it, Paul."

Paul didn't answer for a few seconds. He was thinking hard, and trying to force himself to a decision. He didn't like the idea, but this was the last straw. He was *scared* of this fish, and it had got past the stage where he wasn't willing to admit it. The thing had to go. It *really* had to go.

"No," he told Gemma. "I've got another idea. A better one. In fact. . ." He swallowed. "I think it's the only idea left."

"It's no use," Paul said. "I just can't do it."

He looked at the net, and the fish inside it. The fish gazed back at him, and there was almost a smile of triumph on its face. Then with a sudden movement Paul put the net back into the aquarium and watched as the fish swam nonchalantly out.

"OK," Gemma said in a resigned tone. "I didn't think you could."

He scowled resentfully. "Well, you try it!"

"Oh, I'm not blaming you. I'm no braver. Not in cold blood like that." Then, because she was basically honest, she added, "Or in hot blood, either."

Paul sighed and looked at the collection of objects that he had laid out on the shelf beside the aquarium: a kitchen knife, a hammer, a screwdriver. . . His stomach turned over at the thought of how he had planned to use them. They'd have worked – oh, they'd have worked, all right, but he simply wasn't like that. He couldn't bring himself to kill the fish.

Though he was in no doubt, now, that it wasn't a fish at all, but something else.

He hadn't discussed it with Gemma, but he knew she was thinking along the same lines. What had started off as a joke with a spooky edge had turned into something *really* frightening and dangerous. What the fish was –

natural or supernatural, from this world or from somewhere unimaginable – Paul couldn't begin to guess. But it had latched on to him, and, as he had discovered today, it wasn't about to let go. The unpleasant thought occurred to him that, even if he had had the nerve to try to kill it, the attempt might have gone horribly wrong. After all, a fish that could transport itself up flights of stairs, through solid fridge doors, and back from the beach to this house, had *very* unnatural powers.

And that was to say nothing of the pork chops, the heron, and a terrier called Dinky.

The fish was swimming slowly, contentedly around the aquarium. It looked half asleep, and very smug into the bargain. Little wonder, Paul thought bitterly. It had won its latest battle of wills with him, hadn't it? Just as it had won all the others.

As if from a great distance, he heard himself speak.

"I'll take the tank to my room."

"What?" Gemma stared at him.

He shrugged. "It's the only way to stop Mum and Dad asking awkward questions. If I leave it here, they'll soon see what's happened, but if it's in my room they probably won't notice."

Gemma saw his point, but she wasn't happy. "You've got to sleep in there," she said uneasily. "What if—"

"Don't." Paul cut her off. If he followed that train of thought, he'd lose his nerve. "I'll be all right. It seems . . . well, it seems to *like* the aquarium. So as long as I give it plenty to eat, I don't think it'll cause any trouble."

"What are you going to feed it on?"

Paul didn't want to think about that, either, but he tried to sound confident. "I'll work something out. Don't worry, Gem. It'll only be for a few days. I just need some time to think."

It was three o'clock in the morning when Paul's thinking led to a new and horrendous realization.

He had hardly slept at all. First, he was afraid of having another bad dream like the one the previous night. Secondly, there was the aquarium, now installed in his room. He had put it as far away from his bed as possible, and it was covered by a piece of metal mesh weighted down at all four corners. But for all the precautions, he was unpleasantly aware that it was there – or rather, that its occupant was. He could almost feel the fish staring at him, and he had left his bedside light on, just in case – though in case of *what* was something he preferred not to think about.

So there he was, trying (and failing) to concentrate on a book, when the awful thing struck him. He had been remembering the stallholder at the fairground, who had started all this trouble, and suddenly he thought: *Hang on – how many OTHER people won fish that day?*

The book slid from Paul's fingers and he sat up in bed, shocked. Prize idiot that he was, it hadn't occurred to him before! The creepy little man had had lots of fish on his stall. And that hoop-la game had been all too easy. There was no way that he could have been the only person to win.

So what had happened to all the other people who took a "luvly, lively little fish" home with them?

Paul realized that his mouth had opened in a dumb, round "O" like one of his shubunkins (ex-shubunkins, he corrected himself queasily). He shut it hastily, and did some rapid guesswork.

There hadn't been *that* many people at the fair, and most of them were more interested in the rides than in a run-down and old-fashioned hoop-la. But the man must have had *some* other customers.

Even a few would have been more than enough.

He looked at his clock and was dismayed to see how early it was. He needed to talk to Gemma, but if he woke her up now, she'd be too furious to listen. He would simply have to wait.

He tried to settle down and get at least a bit of sleep, but it was impossible. He tossed and turned restlessly and at last, at half-past five, he gave up. If Gemma didn't like being disturbed, she would have to lump it. This was an emergency.

It was odd, Paul thought as he dressed, that though parents minded very much how late you went to bed, they couldn't care less how early you got up. He tiptoed to Gemma's room, opened the door without knocking, and went in. His sister was sound asleep, snoring slightly, and Paul shook her shoulder.

"Gem! Gem, wake up!"

"Unnzzh?" Gemma rolled over and opened her eyes. "Whasser . . . *Paul?* What time is it?"

"Never mind that," Paul said. "I've got to talk to you!"

She grumbled when she looked at her watch, but Paul cut across her and told her about his awful thought. It took a minute or two for it to sink into Gemma's drowsy mind, but when it did she was as horrified as he had been.

"Oh, no! I didn't even *think* about that!"

"Me, neither. We've got to do something, Gem."

"Too right." She rubbed the last traces of sleep from her eye, then blinked. "Your fish – it's still there?"

"Yes. Worse luck!"

"Hmm. Well, look, give me a sec to get dressed and let's talk about it downstairs."

She joined him in the living-room a few minutes later, and when she came in there was a hopeful look on her face.

"Paul, I've had an idea. Why don't we put an ad in the local paper, asking anyone else who won a fish to get in touch with us?"

Paul's eyes lit with interest. "That way we

might at least find out how many there were. . ."

"Exactly. And if other people have had trouble, well – we might be able to join forces and find a way to get rid of *all* of them."

It made sense, Paul thought. Sometimes, he almost believed Gemma had a brain.

He fetched a pen and paper, and they drafted the advertisement out together. It wasn't easy. The difficulty was in saying enough to get the message across, but not so much that the ad would look like a joke. But at last they agreed that they had it about right.

The ad ran:

DID YOU WIN A GOLDFISH? Brother and sister who won an unusual goldfish on the hoop-la stall at the Bank Holiday Fair urgently want to contact anyone else who won one, to swap important information. Please ring and ask for Paul or Gemma.

"We'll have to put our phone number," Paul said. "God knows what Mum and Dad are going to think when strangers start ringing up!"

"*If* they start ringing up," Gemma pointed out gloomily.

"Don't say things like that!" Paul had horrible visions of what might have happened to the rest of the unsuspecting fish winners. "We'll have to make up a story to put Mum and Dad off the scent. The paper doesn't come out till Tuesday; we'll think of something by then."

"And when it does come out," said Gemma, "let's just hope we get some replies – and quickly!"

8

Paul and Gemma just got their ad to the local paper's office in time for the next deadline. Paying for it took quite a chunk out of the money they had between them, but they agreed it was worthwhile. Now, all they had to do was wait.

Waiting, though, promised to be far from pleasant. To begin with, they had the problem of stopping the fish from making any more mischief. The best way to keep it happy, they thought, was to make sure it was well fed. Paul had plenty of fish-food, but something that could devour – well, never mind; they both knew what sort of things it had devoured – was hardly going to be satisfied with that. So they dug into their pockets again and bought as much cheap meat from the butcher as they could afford. They couldn't put it in the fridge, in case Mum noticed, so they hid it in Paul's room. Gemma said she hoped it wouldn't go off. Paul said he hoped it would; with any luck it might poison the fish.

Gemma's eyes widened. *"Poison. . ."* she said, in the voice of someone who had just had a wonderful revelation. "It's worth a try, Paul! It really is!"

But Paul shook his head. "No. I think we should keep it alive now, until we get some answers to our ad." He paused. "Besides, what if it didn't work? It might . . . *provoke* the fish."

"Ah," said Gemma. "You mean, it would look for revenge?"

"Exactly. And I've got to sleep with it in my room."

Gemma nodded, understanding. "Pity, though." Her face fell.

"It was a good idea," Paul said, trying to cheer her up. "And we go back to school on Monday. That'll help take our minds off it."

She grimaced. "We've still got to get through the weekend!"

If the weekend didn't live up to their very worst fears, it certainly came close.

Paul had taken every precaution he could to make sure that the fish stayed safely in the tank. The fish, though, had other ideas.

Dad was the first person to find it where it shouldn't be. On Saturday afternoon he was washing the car, whistling cheerfully as he sloshed soapy water from a bucket over the paintwork. Dad was very proud of his car, and the Saturday wash was a regular ritual that he thoroughly enjoyed.

Until, as he dipped his sponge into the bucket, something grabbed hold of it from under the water.

Dad stopped whistling, frowned, and tugged at the sponge. For a moment the something tugged back. Then suddenly the sponge came free – with a large chunk bitten out of it.

Dad stared into the bucket in disbelief. And the fish stared back at him.

Luckily, Mum was out and Dad was more inclined than she was to see the funny side of things. He thought, of course, that Paul had put the fish in the bucket as a joke. "All right," he said, "very good, but don't do it again or I *will* tell Mum next time."

But despite the laughs, Paul could tell Dad was uneasy. He never did find the missing chunk of sponge. And that fish . . . well it was growing unnaturally fast, wasn't it? Though Dad didn't actually say that, Paul could see him thinking it.

Paul and Gemma put the fish back in the tank, and this time Paul got some metal clips to hold the mesh down, as well as the weights. The fish ate another large piece of meat. (Strangely, they never actually *saw* it eating. The meat was simply gone next time they looked.) Then it began to swim lazily around.

"It looks pleased with itself," said Gemma darkly.

"Fish's faces don't have expressions." Paul didn't sound convinced, though. He had tried to tell himself time and time again that those goggling eyes and the mouth dumbly opening and shutting couldn't possibly show feelings like pleasure or smugness. But it was becoming harder and harder to believe. At this moment for instance, the fish had a look that was downright nasty. Evil, in fact. Paul had never used that word to describe it before. Now, however, it seemed horribly accurate.

"Gem," he said, "I couldn't . . . well, I couldn't sleep on the floor in your room tonight, could I?"

Gemma's gaze slid sideways to meet his. "Yes," she replied. "I hoped you'd ask. I've been worrying about you alone with it in here. If we're both in the same place, I'll feel safer, too."

Paul had a nasty feeling that being in the same place wouldn't make a lot of difference. If the fish *did* decide to do something unpleasant, one wall wasn't likely to be much of an obstacle to it. But he didn't voice his thoughts to Gemma.

The fish, however, behaved itself that night. In the morning it was still in the tank, though Paul was certain that it had grown a bit more.

All was still well by mid-afternoon, when Mum announced that as the weather was so lovely they would have tea outside. The garden table and sunshade were set up, and everyone trooped out with plates of sandwiches and cake. Dad grabbed the best recliner and lay back with a satisfied, "A-a-a-ah!" while Bella (after deliberately knocking over Gemma's glass of cola when no one was looking) started making a mess everywhere with strawberry jam. Within minutes there was jam all over the grass as well as on her hands, face and T-shirt. Then, cheeks bulging as she munched on her fourth sandwich, she wandered over to the bird-bath.

Only Gemma saw her pull off a piece of sandwich and drop it into the water, and as it was her job to clean out the bird-bath when it got mucky, she was furious.

"Bella!" she snarled. "Take that out!"

Bella turned round, pulled a hideous face, and dropped a second piece of sandwich in.

"*Bella!*" Gemma got menacingly to her feet.

"Feeding the birds!" said Bella defiantly.

Mum, who had shut her eyes and was feeling deliciously lazy, said, "Stop quarrelling, you two."

"Mum, she's putting jam in the bird-bath!" Gemma protested.

"Well, it won't do any harm. The birds'll probably like it."

"Might stop them eating my fruit before I can pick it," commented Dad.

With an exasperated sigh Gemma strode across the grass to pull Bella away from the bird-bath. She would have liked to shove the little wretch's face in it, she thought, jam and soggy leaves and all.

"Go away, pest! Go and find something else to wreck." She barged Bella aside and put her hand in the bird-bath, feeling for the lumps of sandwich. The bath was quite deep in the middle, and Dad had overfilled it this morning so that her hand went in almost to the wrist. She felt something solid, slithery. *Yuk!* If Mum wasn't around she would have made Bella eat this; that'd teach her.

She grasped at the sandwich – and yelped aloud as it wriggled out of her grasp.

Paul and Gemma didn't even try to work out how the fish got into the bird-bath. They had given up asking themselves questions like that; there simply weren't any rational answers. Instead, they resigned themselves to going through the whole rigmarole of another row with Mum about *whose* idea it was and *why* ey had done it and *what* they thought they were playing at. This time, though, she wasn't really angry. She only said the whole thing was silly and childish and she would have thought the joke had worn a bit thin by now. Dad agreed with her, but to Paul and Gemma's relief he kept his promise not to tell Mum about the bucket incident yesterday. Paul fetched his net, the fish was put back in the tank, and no more was said about it.

Again, the fish stayed put overnight, and on Monday morning Paul and Gemma were almost pleased to go back to school. Even if out of sight wasn't exactly out of mind, at least they didn't have to know what the fish was getting up to in their absence.

"Right now I don't even *want* to know," Gemma said feelingly as they got off the bus outside the school gates. "It can wreck the house, eat Bella and sprout fangs and wings for all I care, just so long as I don't have to see it doing it!"

They started to walk up the drive and Paul suggested thoughtfully, "We couldn't keep it at school, could we? You know, in the little kids' pets corner?"

"Oh, great!" Gemma rolled up her eyes.

"And have to explain to Mrs Randall how come all the gerbils and stick insects and things have suddenly disappeared? Not to mention a few teachers, if it got the taste for them?"

"Oh. No, I suppose it's not a good idea, is it?" Though Paul could think of a teacher or two who wouldn't be missed. . .

"It is *not*," said Gemma firmly. "It's no good, Paul; we can't even think of dumping it on someone else. We've got to get rid of it properly. Let's wait till our ad comes out, and see what happens then."

To their enormous relief, there was no more trouble that day or the next. By Tuesday the meat they had bought was looking a bit the worse for wear, but the fish still seemed happy enough to eat it. And it stayed put.

Paul was still sleeping in Gemma's room at night, tiptoeing in once Mum and Dad were in bed and wouldn't know what was going on. The floor was hard and uncomfortable even with two duvets underneath him, and Gemma snored, but he made the best of it, and only got told off twice for dozing off in lessons.

On Tuesday afternoon they were both

feeling nervous as they sat on the homeward bus. The local paper had come out that morning, and they were trying not to think about whether there would be any replies to their ad. They had asked a few cautious questions at school, trying to find out who else had been to the Bank Holiday fair. But it seemed that hardly anyone had, and even the few who did go hadn't encountered That Man and his "goldfish".

Neither of them said a word as they walked to their house. Mum was coming downstairs as they opened the front door. She stopped, giving them a strange look.

"Ah," she said. "You're back."

That was fairly obvious, Paul thought. "Yes, Mum," he said.

"Well, you'd better have a look at the 'phone pad. There are some messages for you." Mum was looking distinctly suspicious. "You're very popular all of a sudden."

"Er. . ." Gemma began, but Paul managed what he hoped was a casually cheerful grin. "Oh, right. Thanks, Mum."

"I didn't know you had all those friends," Mum probed. "Chris, and Sally, and Peter . . .

I've never heard of any of them. I hope you're not up to something."

"No, it's . . . um . . . a school thing. A project we've all got to do. Really boring."

"Oh. Well, if you've got to ring them all back, don't be on the 'phone for hours. It's Dad and I who have to pay the bill, remember."

"All right. Thanks."

Mum gave him another Look as she disappeared into the kitchen, and Paul and Gemma ran to the 'phone.

The names and numbers were on the pad. A full page of them.

And this was just the first day.

9

"Eight," Paul said wonderingly. "Eight people already – all complete strangers!"

"And every one of them's having the same problems as us." Gemma chewed the end of her pencil and stared at their newly-made list. "I wonder how many more there'll be?"

Paul didn't answer. He had tried to remember how many fish the man at the hoop-la stall had had, but he couldn't. All he knew was that it seemed like a lot. And that didn't help in the least.

With Mum out of the way, they had phoned all the numbers on the list. The people they rang couldn't say too much because of parents listening, but what they did say was enough. Yes, they'd all won fish. Yes, they were all having trouble – *big* trouble. So on Friday, after school, they were all going to meet at the harbour for what had been dubbed a Think Tank.

Gemma said that Friday was a long way off, and a lot of unpleasant things could happen before then. Paul, though, argued that they had to allow time for more replies to come in.

"The more of us who can get together at the same time, the better," he said. "Some people might not even see the ad until later in the week."

Gemma saw his point, but she still wasn't entirely happy. "Well, if we've got to wait, we've got to," she said. "I just hope the fish will wait, too."

Paul moved back into his own bedroom on Thursday night. He'd hardly had any sleep all week, and decided that he couldn't stand the discomfort of Gemma's floor any longer. His weariness had brought no end of trouble at school, and even Dad was starting to notice how often he was yawning. So, with only one more night to go before the Think Tank, he decided to risk sleeping in his own bed. The fish had been quiet for days. It seemed perfectly contented. Nothing was going to happen.

At three o'clock in the morning, he was woken by a noise.

Paul opened his eyes, blinking blearily at the dark. He had wanted to leave his bedside light on, but had told himself crossly that that would be stupid and childish. He wasn't a little kid.

Only now, he suddenly felt like one.

His heart thumped uncomfortably as he tried to work out exactly what the noise had been. He thought he had a vague memory of it, but he couldn't be sure, because it had stopped before his brain started to work properly. A sort of . . . *wet* sound . . . like a splash?

Paul sat bolt upright, feeling goosebumps breaking out all over his skin. A splash. *Yes!* he was certain of it now!

Then he heard another noise – very faint, very furtive. As if something was moving cautiously across the bedroom floor. Slithering slowly but surely towards his bed. . .

Paul's heart gave a colossal lurch and he clapped a hand over his mouth to stop himself from screaming. With the other hand he groped frantically for the lamp. Where was it, where *was* it. . .? His fingers found the switch, pressed it . . . and with a sinister *pop!* the bulb fizzed out.

Paul felt as if he had turned to stone. He couldn't move, couldn't breathe, couldn't even think. All he knew was that he was alone in the dark, and something he couldn't *see* was sliding and writhing over the carpet towards him. He wanted to yell for Dad, Mum, anyone. But he couldn't make a sound.

Help! Oh, help, help! Paul's mind churned with terror as he screamed silently inside himself. He knew what was creeping towards him – there couldn't be any doubt. What would happen when it reached him? What would it *do*?

And, came the hideous thought, how big was it now? It sounded *huge*. . .

Suddenly, something in Paul snapped. He would never know whether it was bravery or sheer panic that drove him, but he sprang upright and took a flying leap from his bed, as far as he could. Momentum carried him forward in a teetering run (*did he tread on something squishy as he went? Oh no, please, no, he'd only imagined it!*) and he crashed against the door. For a second or two he scrabbled frantically, then his hand thumped the switch of the overhead light.

A brilliant glare flooded the room, and Paul spun round. Through screwed-up eyes he looked at the floor.

There was nothing there. Nothing at all.

Paul searched every inch of the carpet, just to make sure. He looked under his desk. He took his torch and shone it under the bed. But there wasn't even the smallest trace of a wet mark.

At last he stood up, feeling very foolish. He must have been dreaming – that was the only answer. A bad dream, like the one the other night; only this time his imagination had carried on rioting after he woke up. *Idiot!* he thought.

Leaving the light on (well, it wouldn't hurt, would it?) he started to get back into bed, then stopped again as he realized that there was one horribly obvious thing he hadn't checked.

Very slowly, Paul turned his head to where the aquarium stood.

The mesh that he had so carefully clipped and weighted down stood neatly propped against the glass side.

And the aquarium was empty.

Gemma was so surprised to be woken in the middle of the night that she didn't grumble once. She only listened in dismayed silence as Paul told her what had happened.

"And you're sure it's gone?" she asked when he finished. "*Really* sure? You didn't dream that as well?"

"You can come and see for yourself," Paul said. He shivered. "In fact I don't think, now, that I dreamed any of it. Including the bit where I heard something creeping towards me."

Gemma licked her lips nervously. "Where on earth do you think it might be?"

"I don't know. But I think we ought to find out."

She nodded. She didn't like the idea of a dead-of-night hunt through a dark, silent house but Paul was right. They had to find the fish, if they could.

If it didn't find them first. . .

They ventured out on to the landing. Though neither said so, they would both have given a lot to be able to switch the stairs lights on. But that might have woken Mum and Dad or, worse, Bella. So they took their torches and, by the glow of the wavering beams, tiptoed towards the bathroom, which seemed the most obvious place to start.

"It always finds its way to liquid of some sort," Gemma whispered as they eased the door open. "Or at least, it has so far."

"Let's hope it hasn't changed its mind this time." Paul tried not to think about the purposeful slithering sound across the floor of his room.

They entered the bathroom, eased the door shut behind them, and Gemma pulled the light cord. Everything looked perfectly normal, even down to Bella's toy submarine, which she had deliberately left lying where it was likely to trip someone up. Pity the submarine wasn't a real one, Paul thought, complete with torpedoes. . .

There was no water in the bath or basin. They looked in the airing cupboard and the wall cupboard, then Paul took a deep breath and grasped hold of the loo lid. He snatched it up, half expecting the fish to leap out at him with a glitter of gnashing teeth. It didn't. There was nothing there.

"Well," Gemma said, her voice wavering between relief and disappointment, "it isn't in *this* room."

Paul pushed away a momentary, crazy impulse to turn the taps on. That really *was* nuts; the fish wasn't going to magically erupt out of one of them. They switched off the light and went back to the landing.

"Where now?" Gemma whispered.

Paul chewed over possibilities. "We'd better not go near Mum and Dad's room, or Bella's. I vote we look downstairs."

"OK." Gemma paused. "I want to go to the loo."

"Well, go, then."

"You'll wait for me, won't you? You won't leave me up here on my own?"

"All right, all right! Go on, hurry up." Paul almost added, "Mind the fish doesn't get you!" but the tease wouldn't have been funny.

Gemma went back into the bathroom and he

waited, fidgeting from foot to foot. She seemed to be taking a long time. It was all right for her – she could have the light on in there. He only had his torch, and the battery was going flat. The beam had a yellow tinge and kept flickering, and when he shone it down the landing it didn't even reach as far as the stairs. If anything were to come up the stairs right now, he thought, he wouldn't even see it until it was almost on him. . .

"*Gem!*" He pressed his mouth to the bathroom door. "*Hurry up!*"

"*Ssh!* All right, I'm coming!" The door opened and Gemma appeared. "Sorry," she added. "I was looking out of the window."

"What on earth *for?*"

"I thought I heard a noise in the garden."

They padded along the landing and Paul said, "It was probably Sammy or a hedgehog."

"Or the fish."

He looked quickly at her. "What sort of noise was it?"

"I'm not sure. Sort of . . . rustly."

"Not slithery?'

"No."

"Oh. Cat or hedgehog, then." Which meant

the fish was probably still in the house. . .

They started cautiously down the stairs. Paul's torch was getting dimmer and dimmer; it was all but useless now, and they only had Gemma's to show them the way. She probed from side to side, shining the beam over the stairs, into corners and even across the ceiling. Shadows lurched and jiggled, but nothing else moved. Nothing *solid*.

They reached the hall. A quick check of the living-room told them all was well in there, and as they came out Gemma said, "The kitchen, then."

"Yeah. Looks like it." The trouble was, Paul thought, there were so many places in the kitchen where the fish could hide. There were liquids in the fridge, the washing machine, the coffee percolator. Just about anywhere, in fact. It might seem barking mad, but after all the things that had happened over the past week he wouldn't be shocked or even surprised by anything any more!

The fridge first, he told himself. At least everything in there had a lid on it. His nerves jangled as he opened the door – but, as with the bathroom, nothing jumped out at him. Exhaling a thankful breath, he started to look for any tell-tale signs, like missing or half-eaten food.

Gemma was lifting lids off saucepans and peering into them. She had reached the last one, and Paul was just closing the fridge door again, when a dog started barking somewhere outside.

"That sounds like Gonzo," Gemma said. Gonzo was a large, friendly mongrel who belonged to neighbours three doors away. Suddenly another dog joined in, in a series of high-pitched yaps.

"And that's Ming-Ming, Mrs Lewis's Peke." Paul went towards the door. "What on earth's upset them?"

There were other noises now: more dogs, a cat yowling, even seagulls squawking raucously from the rooftops. The Pekinese, Ming-Ming, sounded hysterical, and the normally good-natured Gonzo was mixing snarls in with his barks.

"Oh, no!" Gemma gasped. "Paul, you don't think it could possibly—"

She didn't get any further. The barkings and yowlings and squawkings suddenly swelled to a crescendo, drowning out her voice.

And from upstairs came a shriek as loud and shrill as the games teacher's whistle, as Bella screamed at the top of her voice.

10

"It was only a bad dream." Mum looked up from where she was bending over Bella's bed. "There, Bella, there's nothing to be frightened of! The nasties have all gone away now, and Mum won't let them come back!"

Paul and Gemma, standing in the doorway, exchanged looks. Paul's said clearly: *Bad dream, huh?* while Gemma's said: *I don't believe it, either.*

Bella had stopped crying now, though her face was still scarlet. The extraordinary animal clamour outside had stopped, too – in fact it had cut off abruptly an instant after Bella screamed, which Paul and Gemma thought very strange indeed.

"What was her dream about, Mum?" Gemma asked.

"Oh, I don't know. Something to do with a seagull, I think, though I couldn't make much sense of it. Better not talk about it in front of her, Gem; we don't want to set her off again. Go back to bed. You too, Paul."

Mum obviously hadn't heard any of the racket outside, Paul thought. What had caused it – and why had it stopped so suddenly? He was sure there must be a connection with Bella's "dream". And he was equally sure that the fish had something to do with it.

Mum had moved to the window. "The night's turned chilly," she said. "I'll just shut this, and then—"

She stopped. She stared. Then her voice rose in a cry of revolted horror. "Oh, my God! What's *that*?"

Paul was across the room in four strides. Mum had shrunk back from the window and he pushed past her to see what was up.

There was something lying on the outside window sill. At first glance it looked like a pile of grubby grey rags. But then Paul saw that there was wet, pulpy redness among the grey, and a round yellow eye, cold and lifeless, was staring up at him from the middle of the heap.

"*Uggh!*" Paul felt nausea churn in his stomach. The horrible mess was – or had been – a seagull. Whatever had killed it had eaten more than half of the corpse, and all that was left now was a blood-soaked bundle of bones and feathers, topped by the remains of the head. It was *gruesome*.

In a horrible flashback, Paul remembered the heron.

"Take it away!" Mum garbled through the hand she had put over her mouth. "Get it out of my sight or I'll be sick!"

Bella started to howl and Dad, who had been hanging around on the landing, came hurrying in wanting to know what was going on. Paul pointed wordlessly at the seagull and Dad made a disgusted noise and went to fetch a bucket. Bella was taken out of the room while the mess was cleared up and put in the dustbin, and Mum, recovering, fetched the disinfectant.

"That cat!" she said as she scrubbed the sill. "Oh, how *repulsive!*"

"You think it was Sammy?" Gemma asked.

"Of course it was! You know what a hunter he is. He must have carried that thing up from the lean-to roof and got into Bella's room with it. No wonder she woke up screaming!"

It was an explanation of sorts. Mum believed it, anyway. But Paul and Gemma both knew that Sammy couldn't possibly have caught a seagull; they were too big, and their beaks too powerful, for him even to try. No; something else had done this. And it didn't take a genius to guess what.

"Oh well," Paul said to Mum, "Sammy won't want his breakfast today, will he? Not after he's eaten half a gull. I'm going back to bed." He signalled with his eyes to Gemma and she added, "Me, too. Goodnight, Mum."

"I can't see anything good about it!" said Mum furiously. "Wretched cat! If he ever does this again. . ."

They left her scrubbing and muttering, and escaped to Paul's room.

"Whew!" Gemma shut the door behind her and pulled a face. "That thing was *foul*. How do you think—"

"Don't ask," said Paul. "I don't want to know

the answer. Look, Gem, we've *got* to find the fish! If Bella hadn't woken up when she did, who knows what might have happened?"

Gemma nodded sombrely. "We'd better wait until Mum and Dad are asleep again, and then. . ."

She stopped. She stared across the room. Then she said in a small voice: "Paul. . ."

Paul turned his head, and saw what she had seen.

The metal mesh, complete with clips and weights, was back on top of the aquarium. And in the water, looking as innocent as a new day, was the fish.

"I don't believe it. . ." Paul's voice shook.

"I do," said Gemma. "Oh, I do. In fact I'd believe *anything* of that creature, now."

The fish flipped its tail lazily and drifted from one end of the tank to the other.

"T.G.I.F.," Paul said.

"What?"

"Thank God It's Friday." He hunched his shoulders. "Think Tank day."

Gemma looked alarmed. "Don't talk about it, not here!" She couldn't shake off the feeling that the fish wasn't just watching them now.

She suspected it was listening, as well.

"I think we ought to go back to bed," she went on. "Try and get a bit of sleep—"

"Fat chance!"

"OK, maybe. But we can *try*. Do you want to come to my room?"

Paul shook his head. "I'll be all right here." The fish wasn't going to do anything else, he was certain. It had made enough mischief for one night.

At the door Gemma whispered, "We'll talk in the morning. Try not to even think about it until then."

She was half convinced, he knew, that the fish could read minds as well, and he tried to smile reassuringly. "Stop worrying, Gem! 'Night."

He shut the door and sat down on his bed. The fish was looking at him while pretending not to. Paul picked up a book. He wasn't going to sleep. Better to stay awake and keep watch, just in case.

He made himself more comfortable, and settled down to wait for morning.

11

Not counting Paul and Gemma, fourteen people walked or cycled to the harbour for the Think Tank the following afternoon.

Though he had known how many to expect, Paul still felt a jolt of shock when he saw them all waiting on the harbour wall. He recognized a few faces – they were at his school, though in different years. And all of them had one thing in common: they looked *worried*.

They walked further along the harbour to where there was a shingle strand at the river's edge, and found a quiet spot among the lines of boats drawn up clear of the water, well away from anyone who might overhear them. Then the stories started to come out.

There was Nick, a thin, dark-haired boy with glasses. He had had twenty prize goldfish in his garden pond till the day after the fair. A few days after that, he had realized that there weren't any birds in the garden any more.

There was Sally, tall and blonde, who kept gerbils. Or rather, *used* to keep gerbils. They had vanished one by one, without any trace.

Then there was Pete. Pete liked to eat, but when his Mum accused him of devouring every scrap of food in the kitchen in the space of forty-eight hours, it really wasn't *fair*.

And then there was Hayley, who came with her twin sister, Kay. They had made the mistake of letting their pet budgies out to fly around the living room. Hayley *thought* she had heard squawking, but by the time she went to investigate, it was too late – *much* too late.

Everyone had a similar tale to tell. Once they realized what was going on, they had all tried in various ways to get rid of their fish. Several people had had the same idea as Paul and Gemma, and had brought the fish here to the beach. In every case, when they got home they had found the fish back in their tanks or bowls or ponds, sneering at them – and unmistakably bigger.

A boy called Darren (who had one arm in a sling) had actually tried to kill his fish. He had borrowed a hammer from his dad's toolbox, taken the fish out of its bowl, and, with his eyes shut, brought the hammer crashing down on its head.

When he opened his eyes again, there was a huge dent in the dining table and the fish was lying, unharmed, two centimetres to one side. Darren stared at the fish. The fish stared back at Darren. Then Darren's nerve snapped; he put the fish back in the bowl and went out of the house.

An hour later Darren's rollerblades had skidded on something on the pavement. The fall he took left him with a sprained wrist and a lot of bruises. When he looked at what he had skidded on, he saw that it was the squashed remains of a portion of fish and chips.

Darren had been too scared to make another attempt to kill the fish. Next time, its sense of humour might not be working.

Paul and Gemma listened with growing

dismay to the tales of woe. Everyone had tried to find a solution to the problem but they had all failed dismally. Now, they were running out of ideas.

"The thing is," Paul said, "I think we agree that it's no good just trying to get rid of them somewhere. They've got to *die*."

"Before any of us do," Darren put in glumly.

"Oh, shut up!" Sally nudged him, making him wince as she joggled his injured wrist. Then she added cautiously, "I *did* try to kill my fish, once. Well, sort of."

Paul's felt a twinge of hope. "How?" he asked.

"I put it in the freezer," said Sally. "Then I went away and left it for a bit."

"What happened?"

Sally's face fell. "Not much," she admitted. "When I went back, it was cold and dopey, but it soon recovered."

"Maybe you should have left it for longer," Gemma suggested.

Sally shrugged. "Maybe. But I've got a feeling it wouldn't have made any difference. Besides, I was afraid someone might eat it, and then what?"

"Then nothing, I should think," said Pete. "I mean, a fish that's been chewed into bits can't do very much, can it? And by the time you go to the loo and—"

"All right, we get the idea!" Gemma interrupted hastily.

"Well, I wouldn't want to eat my fish," declared Hayley, and Kay, who always agreed with her sister as a matter of course, chimed in, "Me, neither!"

So that idea was abandoned and they racked their brains for others. The trouble was, whatever they came up with seemed to have snags that they couldn't overcome. This idea was too risky, that one was too complicated – there was always a good reason why things wouldn't work.

At last they had to admit defeat for the time being. It was getting cold, the tide had turned and the river was starting to fill up and lap towards their feet.

"Look," Paul said, "you've all got my 'phone number. If anyone thinks of anything that *might* work, just ring. It's the weekend, so we can get together again if we do get an idea."

There was general agreement to this, and

the group broke up, drifting away in ones and twos. Paul and Gemma were the last to leave. They trudged up the shingle to the harbour wall and started to walk slowly back along the road beyond. Neither of them felt much like talking; there was nothing to say. But they both felt horribly disappointed. All they had achieved, it seemed, was to find out that they weren't the only people with a fish problem. The problem itself still wasn't solved, and didn't look likely to be.

There was usually something interesting to look at along the harbour front – small boats coming in and out, crab or lobster pots being unloaded – but today Paul couldn't have cared less if Long John Silver and five hundred parrots had been doing a song-and-dance routine on the quay. He stared moodily down at his shoes and didn't notice anything around him, until suddenly he bumped into someone.

"Look where you're going!" an angry voice said. A white van was parked at the roadside. Its rear doors were open, and a man balancing several heavy-looking boxes was heading towards the entrance of a restaurant.

"Sorry." Paul got out of the way, and the

man gave him a filthy look before disappearing into the building.

"You were miles away!" said Gemma accusingly.

Paul shrugged. "Who cares?" He glanced back over his shoulder at the restaurant, which was called *Le Joli Bateau*. Daft name: *The Pretty Boat*. From what he'd heard, The Pretty Pricey was more like it. And Pretty Phony, too. It had opened a few months ago, and it was the sort of place that had fake French decor and fake French waiters and a chef who shouted and threw things. And, of course, it specialized in fish.

Fish. . .

Paul didn't realize that he had stopped in his tracks until Gemma, who hadn't noticed either, collided with him.

"Paul, wake up!" she said crossly.

"Uh?" Paul blinked and looked at her.

"I said—"

"Oh. Yeah, right. Sorry."

He didn't say anything to Gemma as they walked on. But he looked back, several times more, at *Le Joli Bateau*. And the inkling of an idea started to take shape in his mind.

* * *

It took Paul all evening, but by bedtime he had got his idea fairly well worked out. There were flaws, and one particularly enormous problem, but if that could be overcome, it might just succeed.

He still hadn't said anything to Gemma. She knew he was up to something and was dying to find out what it was, but Paul managed to put her off the scent. Rather than raise her hopes (and his own, for that matter) too high, he wanted a bit more time. He would see if the plan still made sense in the morning. If it did, then there would be a lot to do before the weekend was over.

12

"It might work!" There was a glint in Gemma's eyes and a growing note of excitement in her voice. "It just might! Paul, if I didn't know better I'd almost think you were intelligent!"

Paul pulled a face at her. "Ha very ha. Seriously though, Gem. If we can just find a way to get them in there. . ."

"Mmm. That's the big snag, isn't it? I mean, we can hardly march into the place and say, 'Hi! have some fish. We're feeling generous so they're a present.'"

"Too right. And if we tried to sell them, they'd tell us to go and jump in the harbour."

"So we've got to find a way of doing it without them knowing." Gemma tapped her fingers on the table. "That man with the van yesterday. If we knew when his next delivery's due—"

"What? And sabotage his load when he's not looking?" Paul shook his head. "Not a chance! He doesn't leave it for long enough. And he parks right on the road, where anyone walking past could see exactly what we were doing. *And* he probably counts the number of boxes. *And*—"

"All right, all right," Gemma interrupted. "I get the point. It won't work. Have you got any better ideas, though?"

"Well, the restaurant doesn't get all its fish from him, does it? They do local stuff as well."

"Ah!" Gemma brightened. "You mean, put our fish in with the local catch? Shouldn't be too difficult. So if we know when the fishermen are going out next—"

"That's easy. We just go down to the harbour and ask."

"Right! Then if we can find out when they're due to come back—"

"Even easier. When the tide comes in, they come in with it."

"Of course!" Gemma enthused. But then her face fell again. "It all sounds great, Paul, but we've still got a problem. A big one."

"What's that?"

She glanced uneasily over her shoulder. Then she whispered, "The fish aren't going to like it."

"Ah." In all his enthusiasm for the plan, Paul hadn't thought about that. Gemma was right, though. The fish wouldn't just sit back – or flop back – and let themselves be dumped in among *Le Joli Bateau*'s next fish order, to be cooked and served up on plates a few hours later. They would object. They would object very strongly. They would *do* something.

And Paul didn't want to imagine what that something might be.

They were both gloomily silent for a minute or two. It had seemed such a good idea, with only a few small details to be sorted out. This, though. . .

Then Paul remembered something.

"Gem. . ."

"Mmm?" Gemma said glumly.

"Do you remember what that girl said? The tall blonde one – what was her name?"

"Sally. No. What did she say?"

"That she tried putting her fish in the freezer, to see if that killed it."

"Oh, right. I remember. It didn't work, though, did it?"

"No-o," Paul's spark of hope, which he thought had gone out, was beginning to flicker again. "But it *did* make the fish dopey."

"Oh. . ." Gemma saw what he was getting at. It was a gamble, and it could lead to hair-raising disaster if it didn't come off. But if a few hours in the freezer made the fish groggy enough, they wouldn't realize what was going on until it was much too late.

"I wonder," Paul mused, "how long Sally left her fish in the freezer?"

"We only have to phone her and ask," said Gemma.

"Yeah . . . yeah, we do. . ." Abruptly Paul jumped to his feet. He was trying not to let himself feel too eager, but his eyes were alight with anticipation. "Gem, you go down to the harbour and find out when the next catch is due in. I'll ring Sally. Then I'll deal with that fish!"

She looked at him with sudden doubt. "What if the fish gives you trouble? Maybe I ought to stay and help."

"I can manage, don't worry. By the time you get back, it'll be safe and snug in the freezer!"

Gemma hesitated. Then: "All right. But . . . be careful, won't you?"

"Course I will!" said Paul confidently.

"It was only for a couple of hours," Sally said. "Like I said yesterday, I didn't dare leave it there any longer in case someone found it."

Just a couple of hours, Paul thought, but it had been enough to make Sally's fish groggy. Maybe if they were left overnight, the cold would at least knock them unconscious.

Suddenly, unexpectedly, he felt a prickling sensation in his spine and neck, as if a kitten was climbing determinedly up his back. Paul jumped and looked over his shoulder, and Sally's voice came tinnily down the phone: "Paul? You still there?"

"Uh – yeah. Sorry." *Someone walking over my grave*, Dad would have said. The prickly feeling was still there, but he pushed it away and tried to concentrate. "Look, Sally, Gem and I have come up with an idea, but we might have to move fast." His spine was positively crawling now. "I – uh –" *Oh, go away, you horrible feeling! Leave me alone!*

"Paul?" Sally repeated.

"Uh – sorry again. What was I saying?"

"About an idea." Sally sounded cautiously hopeful.

"Oh, yes, right. But it's going to need some planning. We'll have to talk to everyone who came to the beach yesterday."

"I'll ring some of them, if you like," said Sally. "If it helps me get rid of that fish, I'll do *anything*."

"Great." Paul was relieved. Sally's help would save time and his parents' 'phone bill. "OK, then this is what you need to tell them. . ."

Half an hour and six more calls later (Sally was dealing with the rest) Paul finally hung up the receiver. Well, that was Stage One under way. Everyone was going to put their fish in the freezer, and leave it there until it was time for Stage Two. If anyone had problems, they would ring up, but if Sally's experience was anything to go by, there shouldn't be any real difficulties.

So why am I sweating? Paul asked himself.

The answer, of course, was obvious. It was all very well to *talk* about putting *the fish* in the freezer, but *doing* it was another matter. Paul wasn't looking forward to the next few minutes. What if the fish somehow knew what he was planning, and had a scheme of its own to make sure he didn't succeed?

Oh, stop being so stupid! he told himself. How could the fish possibly know what was going on? It was upstairs, he was downstairs; and even if the blasted thing had been in the same room, fish didn't even have ears, let alone understand English! He was acting like a scared kid, and there wasn't anything to be scared of! *Do or die,* his brain added, raiding Dad's sayings again. *Nothing venture, nothing gain. Just stop dithering and get on with it!*

He strode out into the hall, up the stairs and along the landing towards his bedroom. Opening the door took some nerve, but he did it and went in.

The fish was in the tank, drifting mildly around with one fin waggling gently. As he looked at it, it occurred to Paul that the creature had been very well behaved for the past few days. In fact, ever since the Think Tank, it hadn't caused any trouble at all, probably because of all that beef, lamb and chicken it was getting, not to mention a nice juicy seagull the other night. It had grown again, too. How big could it eventually get, if left to its own devices? The crawly feeling wriggled along his spine again as he imagined the fish inflated to ten times its present size and just in the mood for a snack. . .

He shoved that idea as far away as he could, and reached for his net on the end of its short bamboo cane. The fish watched him. Carefully, heart thumping, he lifted the weights from the top of the tank and took off the mesh. The fish still watched him. Net in hand, he leaned over the tank. The fish didn't move. *OK,* Paul thought. *Here goes.*

Very, very gently, he lowered the net into the water. The fish didn't even bother to look at it. Right, then. Draw it forward, slowly, steadily; just another couple of centimetres. . .

The fish moved, so fast that Paul didn't even see how it happened. There was a surge of bubbles, then a sharp *snap*. As the bubbles subsided, Paul found himself holding a broken piece of bamboo cane, while under the water, the fish drifted contentedly, with the other end of the cane in its mouth.

Then it wriggled. Its sides heaved. It gulped, once. And the broken net, cane and wire frame and all, disappeared down its throat.

Its eyes swivelled and it looked up at Paul. It was positively *grinning*.

13

Gemma came back from the harbour to find Paul in the kitchen, with his back pressed to the freezer and his face as white as its door.

"Paul?" She stopped, staring. "Whatever—"

"*Shh!*" Paul flapped a hand at her. "Can you hear anything?"

"What sort of anything?"

"In the freezer, of course, where else?"

Gemma didn't see that "where else" had anything to do with it, but she listened for a moment, then shook her head. "No."

Paul heaved a huge sigh and pushed himself away from the door. "OK. It's stopped at last."

"Stopped?" Gemma echoed. "Paul, what's been going on?"

Over a very large glass of cola, which he reckoned he deserved, Paul told her the whole nightmarish story. It had taken half an hour, and all their remaining meat plus six beef-burgers and an entire packet of Kids Kod Krispies (Bella's current food fad) to do it. But finally the fish's appetite was satisfied enough for him to get it into another net (a hideous pink one belonging to Bella). Holding his catch at arm's length, Paul pounded downstairs at Olympic speed, flung the fish straight into the freezer, and slammed the door on it.

Three seconds later, what sounded like World War Three broke out among the chips and vegetables and ice cubes. The freezer rocked as the fish tried to batter its way out, and even with his whole weight thrown against the door Paul only just had the strength to stop it from bursting open. The mayhem went on for what seemed like hours before things started to quieten down, and Gemma had come in just as it finally stopped.

"Whew!" Gemma said when she had heard it all. "What a horror story!"

"Tell me about it!" Paul agreed fervently. "I wish you'd got back earlier!"

"Sorry. But I've got news, and it's good." She took a swig from Paul's glass, without asking. "I saw Mr Jackson, the Harbour Master. You know how chatty he is – he told me everything I needed, and more." She grinned. "Some of the fishing boats are going out after midnight tonight, when the tide turns. They'll be back on the high tide tomorrow lunchtime. And their catch is going to *Le Joli Bateau*!"

Paul's eyes widened with delight. "That's brilliant!"

"Couldn't be better, could it? All we've got to do now is get all the fish together, and slip them in with the catch. Sunday lunchtimes are really quiet around the harbour, so there'll be far less chance of anyone seeing what we're up to."

"Right!" Paul finished his drink and jumped to his feet. "Let's get on the 'phone, before Mum and Dad get back."

They started towards the living-room, and Gemma said, "Talking of Mum and Dad – you know it's their wedding anniversary tomorrow, don't you?"

"Oh, no!" Paul stopped, horrified. "I'd completely forgotten!"

Gemma wrinkled her nose at him. "Well, *I* remembered while I was out. So I got a card."

Dismay changed to relief, and Paul looked sheepishly at his sister. "Gem," he said, "You're a genius!"

By the time the rest of the family came back, it was all arranged. Paul and Gemma had decided that it wouldn't be a good idea if everyone who had come to the Think Tank turned up at the harbour with their frozen fish. A group that size would attract too much notice. Instead, they would all meet in town on Sunday morning, then just four of them – Paul, Gemma, Sally and Nick – would take the fish and, as Nick put it, "do the dirty deed".

Paul's one desperate hope was that Mum wouldn't want anything from the freezer before then. He didn't dare open the door to see how much havoc the fish had created, but he could imagine it, and Mum's reaction didn't bear thinking about. The longer that door stayed shut, the happier he would be.

Luckily, Bella demanded pizza for dinner –

"Not a stinky-horrid-frozy thing; I want a *real* one" – and Dad was feeling indulgent. So a delivery was ordered from town, and the freezer wasn't opened. Paul and Gemma wrote their anniversary card, and with the tank in his bedroom blissfully empty Paul slept better that night than he had done for a long time.

In the morning, the good luck continued. Mum in particular was delighted that Paul and Gemma had remembered the wedding anniversary, so that put them in her good books. Dad was pleased and secretive about something – a surprise treat for Mum, they guessed – and even Bella wasn't being as obnoxious as usual.

There was one bad moment when, with Mum out of the way, they opened the freezer. They expected to find a scene of total chaos – but they didn't. The fish was in there all right, still and rigid and ice-cold to the touch. But there was nothing else in the freezer – not so much as an ice-cube. And the fish was *definitely* bigger.

Gemma stared at the emptiness and started to say, "What's Mum going to—"

"Don't," Paul interrupted. "We'll face that

one when we have to." He had a cool-bag ready; gingerly he picked the fish up and put it inside. It only just fitted, and he snapped the bag shut quickly. "Come on," he added. "Let's get out of here while we can."

Dad was in the hall. Seeing the cool-bag he said, "Off to the beach, are you?"

"Uh . . . yes, Dad."

"Well, don't be back late. I want you two here in good time for this evening, all right?" Dad winked, and with a promise that they wouldn't forget, Paul and Gemma made their escape.

The meeting in town went so smoothly that by the time they were cycling towards the harbour with Sally and Nick, all with ice-cold carrier bags hanging from their handlebars, Paul was getting jittery. Everyone had turned up, everyone had brought their fish, and every fish was frozen rigid, incapable of doing anything. There were a few hairy-moment stories to tell, but no major disasters had happened, and now only one more stage of the plan remained.

Arriving at the harbour, they saw the fishing boats. They had just come in on the tide, and piles of boxes were being stacked on the quay wall.

"Great!" Gemma jumped off her bike and leaned it against a nearby bench. "We're right on time!"

"Looks like a good catch," Paul added. "We'll wait here till they've finished unloading, then move in."

"Are you sure we'll be able to do it?" Sally asked dubiously. "I mean, they might leave someone on guard, or something."

Paul laughed. "Not a chance! As soon as they've finished, they'll all be off to the pub. Wait and see."

They didn't have to wait long. The fishermen were thirsty, so they didn't waste any time. In less than half an hour the unloading was complete, and the men vanished like smoke, leaving the boxes ready for collection.

Paul looked round. There were only three people in sight and they looked like tourists. "Right," he said. "Come on!"

Carrying the bags of fish and trying to look casual, they sauntered towards the quay. Most of the catch was stacked in one heap. But there was a second, smaller stack a little way away. These boxes were different – they had properly printed labels, and when they looked, they saw that the labels read *Le Joli Bateau*.

"These are the ones," said Nick. "Looks as if the restaurant have supplied their own." He lifted a lid. "They've even got ice in them."

"Brilliant!" Paul crowed. "No one'll think it's weird that our fish are so cold!" He picked a fish out of the box and examined it. "I think these are—"

"Oh never mind what they are, Paul, let's just get them out and put ours in!" Gemma interrupted, fidgeting uneasily from one foot to the other. She was frightened that any minute now the bags would start to squirm.

"OK, OK." Paul and Nick plunged their hands into the first box, emptied it quickly and tipped out their own bags. Their fish were a lot bigger; the box only held six of them, and hastily they began on the second. The fish didn't move – they were still frozen enough not to be *able* to move – but Paul had the unpleasant feeling that they were all glaring at him.

With Sally helping and Gemma keeping a

125

lookout for anyone coming, they managed to cram all the fish into three boxes. The last lid went back on, and the packers straightened up with sighs of relief.

"What about the ones we've taken out?" Nick asked.

"There's some empty crates there – let's shove them in and put them with the other stack."

They re-packed the fish, and as the last ones went in and Paul wiped his chilled, scaly hands down his jeans, Gemma hissed, "Someone's coming out of the restaurant!"

"Quick!" Paul said. "Sit on the harbour wall and pretend to admire the view!"

They perched in a row on the wall and tried to look nonchalant as two men approached from *Le Joli Bateau*. The men glanced at them briefly; Paul whistled, gazing at the river, and Sally pointed to the sky and said loudly, "Ooh look, a seagull!"

The men picked up the boxes and turned away. Four pairs of eyes bored into their backs as they walked off. Everyone held their breath and no one so much as moved a muscle or uttered a sound.

Then, as the men disappeared through the

restaurant's side door, Gemma lifted one hand and, very gently, waggled the fingers.

"Bye-bye, fish," she whispered.

It broke the tension like an explosion, and suddenly there was a four-person mini-riot on the harbour wall.

"We've done it, we've done it!"

"They've really gone!"

"And they'll never come back again-o, they'll never come back again!"

Finally, when the yelling and whooping and high-fives subsided, they flopped back on to the wall, gasping and exhilarated.

"The ones I feel sorry for," Gemma said when she had her breath back, "are the restaurant's customers. Imagine eating those fish. Yuk!"

"Serves 'em right," said Paul. "Anyone who's daft enough to pay their prices deserves all they get!"

Sally stood up. "Well, I'd better get back. Haven't done my homework yet." She raised her eyebrows. "I won't exactly say it was *fun*, but. . ."

"Yeah." Paul grinned. "I know what you mean!"

They started back along the harbour to where they had left their bikes. At the curve in the road, Paul looked back at *Le Joli Bateau*, and grinned.

"Happy eating, suckers!" he said.

14

"Lobsters!" The chef flung his arms skywards. "Where are my lobsters? And my crabs? This is not, I repeat, NOT WHAT I ORDERED!"

The restaurant manager made a sickly attempt at a consoling smile. "Calm down, Jacques! It isn't the end of the world. You can make these into something. . ." He looked dubiously at the opened box of fish. "Something . . . edible."

"EDIBLE?" shrieked Jacques. "You call my creations only EDIBLE?"

"No, no, no!" the manager soothed. "Of course not! You're a genius, of course you are, and whatever you create will be magnificent!" He looked at the fish again. He had the very peculiar feeling that they were staring back at him.

Jacques stamped up and down the kitchen, growling. His name wasn't really Jacques, and he wasn't French. But customers at *Le Joli Bateau* wouldn't be impressed by a chef called Baz who came from Leeds. So Baz had learned to do a good French accent and throw things, and now he actually believed he *was* Jacques. He did cook very well indeed, so the manager didn't mind – except when Baz/Jacques had a tantrum.

"*Mon dieu*, I don't even know what these things ARE!" the chef raved. "How am I supposed to create if I don't know what I'm creating with?"

The manager shrugged. Fish were fish as far as he was concerned. Then his face brightened.

"Call it something Provençale and the clients'll love it," he said. "You know what they're like – provided it *sounds* authentic French, they don't care what's in it."

Baz/Jacques made a snarling noise, but he was beginning to calm down. "Well, at least they're a good size," he admitted grudgingly. "And plump."

"You could do something completely new," the manager suggested hopefully. "I'll make a big splash of it on the menu. Very high price. And we've got a special party booked in tonight." He paused. "It's been a while since I paid you a bonus, hasn't it. . .?"

There was a long silence. The manager could see Baz/Jacques's brain working, calculating. Then, suddenly, the chef exploded, "Yes! I have it!" He started to flap his arms wildly again. "Everyone out of my kitchen!" He started to push the manager willy-nilly towards the door. "Out! I said. Out, out, OUT! I am going to CREATE!"

Paul stared at Dad and gasped, "No. . ."

Gemma couldn't even say that much. She just stared, mouth open, at Dad's beaming face.

"Oh, yes!" Dad was so pleased with himself that he didn't notice the horror in their looks. "As a special anniversary treat, we're all going to have dinner at *Le Joli Bateau!*"

"Me too, so there!" Bella, who had already got her best party dress on, danced up and down behind Dad and stuck her tongue out.

"You two had better go and get ready," Dad went on, still beaming. "No T-shirts and no trainers – make yourselves properly presentable."

They couldn't argue. There was nothing at all they could say without telling Dad the truth, and, as Paul put it as they trailed upstairs, there was about as much chance of him believing that as there was of finding Elvis alive and well and running the local newsagent's.

"We'll just have to get through it somehow," Gemma said. "Maybe if we don't eat anything. . ."

"Don't be daft." Though the idea of what they might have to eat was already making Paul feel queasy. Trouble was, they wouldn't *know*.

"I suppose there's a funny side to it really," he pointed out. "I mean . . . it's a kind of poetic justice, isn't it?

"To us, or to the fish?" But the corner of Gemma's mouth was twitching slightly.

"Well . . . both, I suppose."

There was silence for a moment, then suddenly they both snorted with laughter.

"You are what you eat!" said Paul, quoting yet another of Dad's sayings.

Gemma sniggered. "In that case – *rrrowr!*" She made a mock lunge at him, gnashing her teeth.

He shoved her away. "Come on then. No T-shirts or trainers – let's keep the old folks happy!"

If there was something slightly hysterical about Paul and Gemma's jollity that evening, no one else noticed. They were all shown to their table at *Le Joli Bateau* by an ingratiating waiter who made Paul think of a penguin, and the menu was put in front of them with a flourish.

It had to happen, of course. Mum and Dad both chose "tonight's particular creation", which was called, enigmatically, "Fantasie à la Jacques". It was the most expensive thing on the menu, so Bella wanted it too, and Dad said he was feeling generous so why didn't Paul and Gemma join in and make it five?

"Um . . . no thanks, Dad," Gemma said. "I . . . um . . . I really fancy some. . ." She looked frantically at the menu.

"Mussels," Paul improvised. "We'll have mussels!"

Gemma glared at him. He knew she hated mussels. "Or this – something Provençale—" she suggested, then yelped as Paul kicked her under the table and shook his head. Of course; there was no way of knowing what the *something* was.

"OK." She gave in. "Mussels."

"Fantasie à la Jacques" certainly looked good and smelled wonderful. Mum and Dad said it tasted wonderful, too, and Bella, who could eat like a horse when she wanted to, had to be stopped from licking her plate. Gemma managed to shove most of her mussels into her shoulder-bag when no one was looking, and fell ravenously on her dessert.

Meanwhile, in the kitchen the manager was delighted by the success of the new creation. By the end of the night there wouldn't be a single portion left, and Baz/Jacques had only had one fit of temper, because he said two of the fish were too small. He had ordered them to be thrown "out-out-OUT!" and the manager signalled to one of the staff.

"Sue, chuck these away, will you?" He

handed her a plastic bag with the two fish in it. "Better get rid of them before the Tantrum King comes back."

Sue grinned. "OK." She took the bag and went out of the back door to the dustbins. As she lifted the bin lid, the bag squirmed suddenly. Sue jumped, then peered inside. The fish were *moving*. They were still alive!

"Ohh . . . poor little devils." Sue put the lid back on the bin. It didn't seem right just to leave them to die. She'd put them in the harbour instead – give them a chance.

The tide was low, so Sue scrunched over the shingle and walked down to the river's edge. When she opened the bag, she could have sworn that the fish were both looking at her, and the looks seemed to say, "please help us".

"Poor little devils!" she said again. She upended the bag, and the fish flopped into the water. For a few moments they drifted, and Sue wondered if they were too far gone. But then one gave a flip of its tail. Then the other did the same. They wriggled. Their fins waved. And the next instant they were gone, swimming away into the current.

Sue straightened up, smiling. Then, pleased

with her good deed, she turned and hurried back to the restaurant.

Dad blanched a bit when the bill came, but he didn't grumble about it. It was a special treat, after all. Gemma was thinking longingly of the dessert and wishing there had been more mints with the coffee, when something Mum was saying registered on her brain.

". . . Bank Holiday again before we know where we are. Honestly, there seem to be so many holidays these days, it's a wonder anyone ever gets any work done."

Dad laughed. "Well, it keeps the fairgrounds in business, doesn't it? I suppose the same one will be back in town." He looked at Paul. "Just do me a favour, Paul – if you go again, don't bring any strange fish back next time!"

Paul and Gemma froze in their seats as what he had said hit them like a wet slap.

"N-next time. . .?" Paul echoed feebly.

"The fair – that fish you won." Dad grinned. "No more piranhas, eh?"

"Gemma?" said Mum. "Are you all right? You look very pale."

"I . . . uh . . . I—" Abruptly Gemma

scrambled to her feet. "'Scuse me – got to go to the loo."

"Me, too." Paul rushed out after her. In the passage that led to the loos, they faced each other, horror in their eyes.

"We didn't even *think*. . ." Gemma breathed.

Paul gulped. "He might not be there this time. . ."

"But what if he is. . .?"

There was a deep, cold, hideous feeling twisting in Paul's stomach as he thought about it. "Yeah," he whispered, and there was dread in his voice. "*What if. . .?*"

15

You could hear the bawling voice half-way across the field, above all the shrieking and clanging and banging and blaring music of the fair. For one last, desperate moment Paul and Gemma hoped they were wrong, and that the voice would turn out to belong to someone else. But as they turned towards the sound, hope died. There couldn't be any mistake. There just couldn't.

There he was. Squat and dumpy, with his barrel body and bandy legs, and the grin under the tweed hat that made him look like a shark. He was wearing exactly the same shrieking jacket and clashing check trousers. And he was bellowing out his patter with all the gusty energy of a full gale.

"Win a fish! Win a luvly, lively little fish!"

The hoop-la stall was set out exactly as it had been last time, and Paul and Gemma edged their way towards it. The stallholder didn't notice them; he was too busy shouting. But something else did. A lot of something elses, in fact.

There must have been at least thirty fish, all swimming around in their polythene bags, which were hung up on a wooden rail. They had the same beautiful, marbled-silvery markings, the same exotically feathery tails and fins. They were no bigger – yet – than goldfish.

And every single one of them was *leering* at Paul and Gemma.

"Roll up, roll up, ladies and gents!" the stallholder bawled. "Win a fish! Easy as pie, and only twenty pee a go! Thank you very much, madam, and here's the hoops for your little boy!"

Paul spun round, then grabbed Gemma's arm. "Look!"

She turned, and saw a plump woman with a

small child at the stall. The child threw the hoops. Every one of them hit the mark.

"There we are, son! Told you it was easy-peasy, didn't I?" roared the stallholder. "Have a luvly fish! Any one you like!"

Paul and Gemma could only watch in appalled silence as the little boy trotted away with his mum, triumphantly holding his prize. As they disappeared into the crowd, Gemma said in a small, shaky voice: "There's someone else with one. Over there. . ."

"And another." Paul pointed. "Oh, *no*. . ."

"We've got to do something, Paul!"

"Don't I know it! But what?"

A new customer was at the stall now, and numbly they saw the whole scene enacted over again. Another win. Another fish. Easy as pie.

Paul and Gemma looked at each other. There was only one thing they could do, and they both knew it without the need for words. It was going to be difficult. In fact it would probably be hopeless. But it was the only chance they had.

They sidled away from the stall. The fish stared after them. Though they didn't know it, the stallholder saw them too. He gazed after them for a moment, and his pale, fishy eyes were sly. Then he turned his attention back to his stall.

"There's one." Paul pointed to where a couple with three children were buying hotdogs. Two of the children had plastic bags with fish in them. "Go on. You first."

"No, you," Gemma argued. "You started this, after all."

She was right. Taking a deep breath, Paul walked across to the candy-floss stall.

"Excuse me. . ."

The family all turned and looked at him. The father glared. The mother scowled. One of the children pulled an awful face and the two with fish hid them behind their backs.

"Um . . . sorry to bother you," said Paul, with his heart sinking through his shoes, "but there's something you ought to know. . ."

Back at the harbour, *Le Joli Bateau* was just closing after the lunchtime rush. The town was full of holidaymakers, and the beaches were crowded. It was nearly low tide now, and people were paddling in the rock pools. Some had nets and were fishing or shrimping. Dogs yapped. Toddlers squealed and splashed.

And one man, wading into the sea for a swim, felt something brush against his leg. Something large. It wasn't seaweed. . .

The owner of the hoop-la stall could still see Paul and Gemma. They didn't seem to be having much luck. People didn't want to know; in fact, the last lot had looked downright threatening as they chased the pair off. A grin spread across the stallholder's face. It was not, by any stretch of the imagination, a pleasant grin. Then he opened his mouth, and his gale-force voice bellowed jovially out over the din of the fair: "Win a fish! Win a luvly, *lively* little fish!"

Are they ordinary animals – or are they

Creatures...?

Don't miss

If You Go Down to the Woods

by Louise Cooper

Turn the page and read on

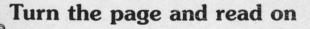

Creatures – you have been warned!

She sat up, curious. As she did so, she realized something else. The sound wasn't coming from outside. It was much closer.

It was in the room with her.

Alex's heart lurched a second time, and her skin started to prickle and crawl. She wanted to turn her head and look around, but she was suddenly too frightened to move. The soft rustling continued. It was a very steady sound. And it was getting closer, as if something was moving slowly but relentlessly across the floor towards her.

Her pulse was pounding like hammers now, and desperately she swivelled her gaze, trying to see into the room's corners. The street lamp showed the dim outlines of furniture, and Alex knew she could easily lose control and believe that those outlines were moving. They weren't, of course. They couldn't be. They weren't alive.

But something in here was. . .

She shut her eyes and forced herself to take a deep breath. This was stupid. Her imagination was running riot and she had to calm down. Just one second, that was all it would take to reach out to the lamp on the table beside her. *For God's sake,* she thought, *it's only a few centimetres away! Do it – just do it!*

With her eyes still tightly shut, her hand shot out. Her fingers touched the lampshade and she almost knocked the whole thing over. A frantic grab saved it and she scrabbled for the switch, fumbling and gasping with the terror of suspense. She felt as if the darkness beyond her eyelids was about to pounce, and a voice inside her screamed in silent fear: *The rustling's getting louder, it's getting louder—*

With a click the lamp came on – and instantly the rustling stopped.

Slowly, Alex opened her eyes. The lamplight seemed glaringly bright and harsh, making her blink as she stared nervously at the room. It was very quiet, and everything looked absolutely normal. There was her desk and chair. Her bookshelf. Her cassette radio. The wardrobe door was closed, as she had left it. Even the bags of panto costumes still lay on the floor where she had dropped them. Alex glanced at the bags, and—

"*Aah!*" It came out as a squeak rather than a scream, which was just as well, as her parents were asleep in the next room. Alex put a hand to her mouth, pushing down half-hysterical laughter and calling herself a prize idiot. It wasn't a small and horrible monster that was glaring up at her from among the bags – it was only the fox-fur wrap! The junk shop carrier had fallen over, tipping some of its contents on to the carpet, and the fur was among them. It was partly hidden behind the other bags, so that only the head showed, and for a moment it had looked so real that it frightened the life out of Alex.

Her laughter dissolved into a snort. The supposedly "eerie" rustling must have been made by the plastic bag slowly uncrumpling itself after it fell over. That was a *really* dumb thing to be scared of!

All the same, though, the fox's head was a bit creepy. She didn't fancy the idea of those glass eyes staring at her all night, so she got out of bed and went to pick the fur up. She'd just shove it back in the bag, out of sight, then maybe she could get some sleep.

The fox fur felt very warm to her touch, and it seemed to smell mustier than before. *Better open the window in the morning*, Alex thought, *or Mum will hit the roof.*

She bundled the fur away. Some feathers from the hat had also come off and spilled from the bag; she gathered them up, wondering how on earth they could have managed to spread themselves so far across the floor. That would mean a tricky glueing job tomorrow. Boring.

Alex climbed back into bed. She took a last look round the room, just to be certain that everything was as it should be. No creeping shadows. No strange noises. *Idiot*. The rustling bag had set her off, and she'd imagined the whole thing.

With the fear gone and her pulse back to normal, she switched the lamp off and settled down.

When the rustling began again, it was very quiet, almost furtive. As if something had learned a small lesson, and was taking the greatest care not to wake her a second time. . .

Goosebumps

R.L. Stine

Reader beware, you're in for a scare!

These terrifying tales will send shivers up your spine: